Where family loyalties and passions collide.

Harlequin Desire brings you Dynasties—delicious, dramatic miniseries that span generations, include an engaging cast of characters and sweep you into the world of the American elite. From luxury ranch retreats to the stages of Nashville, from the sagas of powerful families to the redeeming power of passion... don't miss a single installment of Dynasties!

Dynasties: Beaumont Bay

What happens in Beaumont Bay stays in Beaumont Bay. This is the bedroom community where Nashville comes to play!

Twin Games in Music City by Jules Bennett
—available now
Second Chance Love Song by Jessica Lemmon
—available now
Fake Engagement, Nashville Style by Jules Bennett
—available now
Good Twin Gone Country by Jessica Lemmon
—available now

Dynasties: The Carey Center

The Carey family works hard and plays harder as they build a performance space to rival Carnegie Hall! From *USA TODAY* bestselling author Maureen Child Available September, October, November and December 2021

Dynasties: The Ryders

For this perfect all-American family, image is everything. Until a DNA ancestry test reveals secrets they've hidden for generations... From Joss Wood Available February, March, April and May 2022

Dynasties: The Eddington Heirs

In Point du Sable, this empire is under siege. Only family unity and the power of love can save it! From Zuri Day Available July, August, September and October 2022

Dear Reader,

Hallie Banks is starting to feel...well, a little *beige*. Her identical twin sister is a vibrant pop of color as well as a huge superstar, and now Hannah's life is moving forward while Hallie is stuck behind the scenes. Hallie has never coveted the spotlight, but she wouldn't mind having some unscheduled fun...if only she knew how.

Enter Gavin Sutherland: music attorney by day and playboy by night. At an event where Hallie wears a very un-Hallie-like gown, he mistakes her for her starlet sister and proceeds to mention that Hallie works too much and should cut loose every once in a while. Oops!

Properly challenged, Hallie makes him an offer. She'll help with his design woes if he agrees to teach her how to break a few rules. When our good girl gives in to her attraction and surprises Gavin with a kiss, he surprises her back by suggesting they take this challenge into the bedroom. And that's just the start of the fireworks between these two feisty opposites.

Thank you so much for joining Jules Bennett and me for the Beaumont Bay series. I've had a blast creating these cowboy boot–wearing country boys for you. Be sure to keep in touch by signing up for my newsletter at www.jessicalemmon.com.

Happy reading!

Jessica Lemmon

"You are really shameless, did you know that?"

"I like to think of myself as confident."

If Hallie dared stripping to the skin, Gavin would be forced to do the same. And she loved the idea of calling him on his dare.

Gavin's hands landed on her hips. "You're thinking about it."

"Only because I want to give you a taste of your own medicine."

"Why don't you give me a taste of your lips instead?"

She turned in the circle of his arms, wrapped her hands around the back of his neck and lifted her chin. He lowered his mouth to hers and kissed her, teasing the seam of her mouth with his tongue and then diving in for more.

She didn't care if someone was looking out the window or if paparazzi were lurking in the bushes.

Hadn't she worried about consequences for far too long?

So here she was. *Going for it.*

* * *

Good Twin Gone Country by Jessica Lemmon is part of the Dynasties: Beaumont Bay series.

HARLEQUIN®
DESIRE™

Recycling programs
for this product may
not exist in your area.

ISBN-13: 978-1-335-73505-8

Good Twin Gone Country

Copyright © 2021 by Jessica Lemmon

This edition published by arrangement with Harlequin Books S.A.

For questions and comments about the quality of this book,
please contact us at CustomerService@Harlequin.com.

Harlequin Enterprises ULC
22 Adelaide St. West, 40th Floor
Toronto, Ontario M5H 4E3, Canada
www.Harlequin.com

Printed in U.S.A.

JESSICA LEMMON

—

GOOD TWIN GONE COUNTRY

HARLEQUIN
DESIRE

A former job-hopper, **Jessica Lemmon** resides in Ohio with her husband and rescue dog. She holds a degree in graphic design, which is currently gathering dust in an impressive frame. When she's not writing supersexy heroes, she can be found cooking, drawing, drinking coffee (okay, wine) and eating potato chips. She firmly believes God gifts us with talents for a purpose, and with His help, you can create the life you want.

Jessica is a social media junkie who loves to hear from readers. You can learn more at jessicalemmon.com.

Books by Jessica Lemmon

Harlequin Desire

Dallas Billionaires Club

Lone Star Lovers
A Snowbound Scandal
A Christmas Proposition

Kiss and Tell

His Forbidden Kiss
One Wild Kiss
One Last Kiss

Dynasties: Beaumont Bay

Second Chance Love Song
Good Twin Gone Country

Visit her Author Profile page at Harlequin.com, or jessicalemmon.com, for more titles.

You can also find Jessica Lemmon on Facebook, along with other Harlequin Desire authors, at Facebook.com/harlequindesireauthors!

One

Damn you, Brené Brown.

Hallie Banks tugged self-consciously at the bodice of her dress, fretting over her choice for tonight's soiree. She blamed the TED Talk rabbit hole she'd fallen into last night for her sudden change of heart. Imbued with a second glass of Chardonnay, she had written down several resolutions for the year to come, including the one that inspired her outfit this evening: *stand out in a crowd*.

In the strapless, deep plum–colored dress with her hair pinned into a chignon she'd watched no fewer than five tutorials to master, and with her cleavage front and center, she had done a bang-up job of *standing out*. That bold list summarizing all she wanted to become in the new year had been inspiring in the moment, but in the midst of the crowded rooftop bar, her resolve was beginning to fade.

"If I see you fuss with your gown one more time, Hallie Banks, I'm going to tie your hands behind your back," her grandmother Eleanor reprimanded.

"I'm not fussing," Hallie argued, unable to keep from yanking at the bodice one last time.

"You are so. Now, I didn't bring you here to meet my famous friends so they could watch you having a wardrobe crisis in the middle of their cocktail party." Eleanor Banks was country music royalty, so she did indeed have incredibly famous friends. Friends who could help Hallie with another item on her checklist: *expand client roster.*

Still, she found herself murmuring a defeated, "I should have worn the black dress."

"Nonsense! It's about time you wore something befitting of your personality." Eleanor, dressed in a classy silver-and-white gown decorated with a zillion sparkling beads, certainly didn't have any issues being in the spotlight. Hallie was far less practiced than her superstar grandmother and famous twin sister. Hallie was more a behind-the-scenes girl, and until a second glass of Kendall Jackson Chardonnay and Brené's charming, relatable wit had convinced her otherwise, Hallie had been A-OK with staying *out* of the spotlight.

"There he is!" Eleanor wrapped her arm around Hallie's and leaned closer. "Bernard 'Bernie' Merriweather. You're going to want to shimmy over to his good side because his daughter is Martina Merriweather, and she is currently seeking a new manager."

Her questionable wardrobe choice forgotten, Hallie slipped into business mode, her eyes homing in on Bernie. His daughter Martina was twenty-four years old, six years Hallie's junior, and had recently divorced her manager. Literally. The marriage to the older man who ran the young starlet's career had been quiet, but messy. Gram had shared plenty of details when she'd invited Hallie to this event as her plus-one.

Hallie understood managerial pressures from a unique vantage point. She'd managed her twin sister Hannah's career for as long as she could remember— way before Hannah Banks was famous. Before Hannah had a stylist or a hair guy…or a fan base the size of a small country.

Hallie had put herself in charge of her sister's success, championing her at every opportunity. Now Hannah and Will Sutherland were married and Hallie, while happy for them, felt a little lost. She still managed Hannah's career, but it mostly ran on its own steam. It was time for Hallie to branch out and accept more clients.

"Come on, I'll introduce you," her grandmother said. "Grab a champagne on your way over. It'll give you something to do with your hands."

"I'm okay," Hallie replied, grateful her voice had resumed its usual confident tone. Building a business revolving around superstar clients had come naturally to her, given how her grandmother's fame had been a constant in her life.

Hallie put on a smile as Gram introduced Bernie. The older man turned around, his head dipping to address Eleanor. Just as he was extending a hand in greeting to

Hallie, she caught sight of a broad Stetson shadowing the face of a man on the other side of the bar. A man who'd been hidden by Bernie's tall form until just this moment. And that's when her confidence took for the Tennessee mountains.

Gavin Sutherland.

If there was one man on this planet who could turn her into a bumbling, fumbling, tongue-tied mess, it was the youngest Sutherland brother. She'd known him— of him—for years, but now that Hannah and Will were a couple, Gavin had been in Hallie's circle more than ever. Since she and Gavin had consulted each other on recent contracts, she'd begun noticing all sorts of things about him she hadn't before.

Like the way his gray-blue eyes reminded her of a storm rolling in over Beaumont Bay. Or how his hair, longish and slightly wavy on top when he wasn't wearing a hat, was wrangled into a stylish mess like he'd just rolled out of bed. And then there was the distracting days' worth of growth on his chin and jawline hinting that a charming cad lurked under his finely tailored suit.

Whenever she'd popped into the recording studio she couldn't help lingering while he talked on the phone. Sometimes he'd stand at every inch of his six-foot frame and speak with businesslike authority. Other times he'd lean on his door frame and murmur in a tone that was pure, undiluted sex.

Thoughts like those kept her from feeling truly comfortable around him. A charming playboy like Gavin scared her straight down to her pearlescent-pink painted toenails. Which was why, in a fit of bravado last night, she'd added *Have a drink with Gavin* to her ambitious list.

But now that she'd spotted him smiling at another woman, whose tinkling laugh carried on the air, Hallie's inner warrior shrank back from the front line.

"Hallie." Gram's insistent tone hinted she'd said it more than once.

Jerking her attention away from Gavin, Hallie flashed Bernie her most dazzling smile. "Lovely to meet you, Bernie." She shook his hand, gripping firmly and looking into his eyes. Those were the big three when meeting someone for the first time: lead with a firm handshake, make eye contact and use the person's name.

His perplexed frown melted into a smile. "Dimples! I love dimples. Reminds me of my late wife, Cheryl. God rest her soul."

"She was a godsend." Eleanor took Bernie's hand in her own and they briefly reminisced about his late wife.

When Gram expertly steered the conversation back to business, Hallie let her awareness of Gavin fade into the background. Her most important task tonight was to find another client or two to represent. Beautiful men with knee-weakening smiles were nice and all, but so far outside of her comfort zone she'd need a passport to reach one.

She refocused her attention on the elder in front of her, highlighting what she knew of Martina's career, leaving out the scandal, of course. Eleanor was well practiced at schmoozing, connecting Hannah's successes to Hallie's expertise as a manager.

"And the two of you are an exact match. How fun for you growing up," Bernie commented.

Hallie pasted a well-worn smile on her face. *Oh, yes. Fun, fun.* She loved her twin, but being an "exact match" had its downfalls. She'd learned to foster her own personality at a young age. Hallie was naturally bookish and quiet, extroverted when it came to business, but preferred to blend in with the wallpaper during social affairs. Hannah's commanding presence made that easy since she was so comfortable in the spotlight—onstage or off. As they grew into adults, Hallie became more focused on business and Hannah on entertaining. Hallie prided herself on her work ethic and often worked on Saturday nights, whereas Hannah never shied away from dating.

Recently, though, Hallie had felt a pull to break out of her habits, which were beginning to resemble deep ruts on a beaten path. She longed to do something outrageous, if only to prove to herself she could. She'd lived almost in fear of breaking rules lest she suffer the consequences. At the age of thirty, that seemed silly.

Her vivacious grandmother and Hannah had always put themselves "out there" and their lives were nothing short of magnificent. Why couldn't Hallie have a bit of unscheduled fun, too?

Bernie video-called Martina and introduced Hallie. As she chatted to her prospective client, Hallie reconsidered stepping too far out of her comfort zone. She'd count the follow-up appointment she'd scheduled with Martina her win for the night, which, to be fair, was no small feat. There would be another opportunity to run into Gavin and ask him to have a drink. She'd choose her timing carefully. There was no need to cross *every* item off her list tonight.

Outside in the crisp open air of the rooftop bar, Hallie admired the stars, their shine somewhat diminished against the city lights below. Beaumont Bay, known as *the* Nashville bedroom community, was lively and posh, and yet beautiful and homey. She loved this town.

"Well, darlin', I'm heading home. Great job tonight." Gram pulled on her coat and then hugged Hallie. "It's chilly out here, so don't linger. Don't want you getting sick on me." Her lipstick was in place, her face fresh and eyes twinkling. How did she do it? Hallie had been at the event a few hours and already she was exhausted by the chatter and the crowd.

"Actually, I'm heading out, as well. I can walk you down."

"No, no." Eleanor waved her off. "Stay and have fun. You've made solid connections tonight, but the ones made later are better. Because everyone keeps drinking."

With a wink and a wave, Eleanor picked her way through the bar, offering goodbyes without allowing herself to be waylaid by anyone. She was fabulous. Surely, her fabulous gene would've had to be passed on to Hallie, too, right?

"Let's hope," she told the stars, hearing the scuff of shoes on the concrete patio behind her. A mental tug in the back of her mind whispered Gavin's name, but she quickly dismissed it. He'd stayed at the bar most of the evening—with that stunning woman—so why would he seek out Hallie?

"Nice night," her visitor greeted.

Gavin's voice was smooth and rich like dark chocolate but made her hungry for something far more decadent. She sucked in a shallow breath and spun to greet him. Wow. He looked better up close. Tall and solid and smiling. His gray-blue eyes darker beneath the shadow cast from the brim of his hat. Hopefully the dark night sky muted the tinge of her blushing cheeks.

His smile faltered as he took in Hallie's dress and heels. "Hannah."

The greeting was a splash of cold water onto her rapidly heating pulse. He thought she was Hannah. Which gave Hallie two options. She could either correct him and have what would likely be an awkward, fidgety conversation while she tried to hide her obvious admiration of him, or… She could go along with his assumption and pretend to be her twin sister.

Granted, pretending to be Hannah was a cowardly plan, but it wasn't as if this was the first time they'd bailed one another out of a thorny situation by doing just that. And Hallie, already socially fatigued, didn't have the mental energy to charm the youngest Sutherland son tonight.

If ever.

She pulled her shoulders back and softened her voice, easily emulating her twin sister's smooth cadence. "Hey, Gav. How are you?"

His eyebrows pinched in a show of doubt for a second before he bought the lie. Rocking back on his boot heels, he tucked his hands into his pants pockets. "I thought you and Will had plans tonight."

"We do. We did. I came to, uh—" Hallie racked her brain for a reason her twin might come out tonight "—see Gram. Before Will and I go out."

She schooled her expression, careful not to smile and give herself up—because, dimples—and sipped her champagne. Normally, she knew her sister's schedule like her own, but Hallie's brain was a mangled mess. Being this close to Gavin sent her pulse skittering and her thoughts running in Tasmanian-devil circles.

She'd been mistaken for her twin sister many times before, but never by Gavin. It had to be the dress. He would have expected to find Hallie in basic black or a pantsuit. Never a colorful strapless number. She reached up and tugged the bodice of the dress again, which drew his eyes to her chest. To his credit, he jerked his attention away immediately, clearing his throat before he spoke.

"I thought Hallie would be here. This is the perfect venue for her to meet new prospective clients."

"I know, right?" Hallie nodded in agreement. "I am going to call her the second I leave and tell her to get her booty down here."

Booty? She'd never used the word booty in her life. God, she felt like a grade-A moron whenever he was around. He was all smooth ease and charm, and she was... Well, she was good at spreadsheets. That had to count for something. Unfortunately, flirting was not near the top of the list of things she'd mastered.

How had she convinced herself she'd both show up in this daring dress and invite him to have a drink with her? Brené needed to manage her viewing audience's expectations a bit better.

"Well, it's probably for the best," he said, looking over his shoulder at the crowd inside. "She doesn't like me anyway."

"What?" Hallie squawked.

"Don't try to spare my feelings, Hannah. We both know your sister is not my biggest fan."

Um. So not true. If there was an I-Heart-Gavin fan club, Hallie would be the president.

"She hardly speaks to me. Barely looks at me." He sounded almost stung. How was that possible? Why would Gavin care what Hallie thought of him anyway? "I thought maybe she was in the zone at work functions, but even at your wedding—nothing. You'd think since we're practically family she'd at least make eye contact."

She didn't know what to argue with first. At the wedding, he'd been infatuated with one of the brides-maids and studiously ignoring Hallie. And Hallie and Gavin were in no way "family." Hannah had married his brother, not Hallie. When would the world stop see-ing them as the same person?

"Between you and me, it's probably easier if she and I stay away from each other. Who needs the complica-tion, am I right?" His casual smile had Hallie pursing her lips. He was *not right*. In fact he was *all wrong*.

"On second thought, she's probably too busy man-aging my entire career to dabble in a little party like this," Hallie found herself snapping. She attempted to smooth it over. "You know Hallie."

"Right. Always working," he assumed correctly. "No time for fun."

She didn't like the way that sounded, so she straightened her shoulders and corrected, "She could have a date tonight."

"Hallie? Land a date?" His sharp laugh sent a flood of heat to her cheeks.

Hallie nearly dropped character. She was simmering in a stew of embarrassment and anger, every part of her wanting to point out he was a horse's ass. Did he really believe she was *incapable* of scrounging up a date?

Her mouth set in a soft line, she pulled a calming breath through her nose. What would Hannah say in this situation? "Hallie is an astute professional who wouldn't be caught dead with a date at a business event, let alone flirting at the bar."

She hadn't been positive he'd been flirting earlier, but his raised eyebrows were as good as an admission. Gavin Sutherland charmed every woman who crossed his path, except for the one who liked him most.

"Shit, Hannah, I'm sorry." He palmed the back of his neck. The gesture made him look chagrined and endearing. Or would have if Hallie wasn't so busy feeling insulted. "I didn't mean any disrespect. It's none of my business what Hallie does in her spare time."

She pulled her shoulders back and resisted the urge to say, *Damn straight!*

"But between you and me and the fence post," he went on, "it'd do her good to take a spin in your shoes. Break a few rules. Have some fun."

"Have some fun," she repeated flatly, one eyebrow winging upward.

Misunderstanding her meaning, he answered, "Oh,

I will," before palming her arm in a friendly manner. "Tell Will I said hey."

He filtered into the crowd. Hallie chewed on her bottom lip. She'd stepped out tonight with the intention of talking to Gavin. Boy had she, but not in the way she'd expected. She'd hoped for a drink and conversation, not him being completely stumped as to how she could possibly "land" a date or enjoy herself at a party.

She set her unfinished champagne glass on a table and collected her coat. By the time she pushed the lobby button on the elevator, the doors were closing on a tableau of Gavin smiling fondly at a young brunette at the bar.

Hallie spared him her steeliest glare, deciding to amend her list the second she got home.

Maybe "avoid Gavin forever" should take the number one spot instead.

Two

"Friend of yours?" the brunette sitting on Gavin's left asked as she followed his eye line across the bar. Hannah disappeared behind two closing elevator doors to go home to Gavin's brother and gallivant off to...wherever it was they were going. He found it odd she hadn't mentioned where.

"Sister-in-law," he told the brunette. Alex Lockwood was her name, and she had recently signed with Elite Records. Gavin was acting as her attorney in sponsorship matters, which was good news for her. He knew a lot of wealthy business folk who wanted country music crooners to hock their wares. The young singer was bubbly and crazy talented. She was also young. Very young. She twirled her hair and grinned. Her teeth were so white he reminded himself to call the organic toothpaste company in his contact list about her.

"I thought maybe you'd dated her or something, the way she was looking at you."

"You mean like she wanted to throttle me? I mentioned her twin sister and she took what I said the wrong way." Or, more accurately, he'd said exactly the wrong thing. "You do know who Hannah Banks is, right? Superfamous wife of my brother Will, who owns the record company that signed you?"

Alex's eyes widened. "*That* was Hannah Banks? Oh my God." She sent a remorseful glance to the elevator. "I would love to meet her. I didn't recognize her not wearing sequins and without her hair out to *there*. Celebrities really look different when they are out of their element, don't they?"

"Yeah," he said distractedly. Hannah *had* looked different tonight. After he'd said her name, he thought for a second he'd confused Hallie for her. But he'd never seen Hallie wear a brightly colored, strapless dress. Not to mention he'd felt a misplaced jolt of attraction to the blonde on the outdoor patio, which was super weird. He'd seen Hannah dozens of times dressed to the nines, and she hadn't ever elicited that sort of response from him.

Though, he'd had that sort of response to Hallie once or twice. In passing. Not that he'd have acted on it. If he pursued the more serious of the Banks twins, she'd cut him down where he stood. Even if she didn't, she wasn't for him. Hallie was a good girl. He preferred to keep his relationships easy and short. He doubted

Hallie, if she did agree to date him, would accept those terms. Plus, Hannah was his sister-in-law, which made any entanglement with Hallie a no go. If things ended badly, he'd never escape her.

He chuckled under his breath. How ridiculous was the idea he'd *need* to escape? Hallie barely talked to him, rarely stood next to him. He wasn't joking when he'd told Hannah her twin sister avoided him.

Hannah was signed with Elite now, and with her came Hallie, her manager. Gavin had negotiated several contracts for the superstar, mostly via email with Hallie. On the rare occasion she was in the studio, she'd peer over the black-framed glasses she sometimes wore before rerouting her attention to her iPad. Then she would scuttle off and email him the details rather than talk to him.

He didn't know what he'd done to make her hate him.

"I'll introduce you to Hannah when she's not, ah, busy." Or when she wasn't pissed at him. He didn't mean to laugh at the idea of Hallie having a date, like she couldn't possibly convince someone to go out with her. He knew better. Hallie was gorgeous. If she let her guard down for two seconds, she could easily find several guys who wanted to take her to dinner.

And then he'd had to stick his other foot in his mouth to join the first, hadn't he? He'd been sincere when he'd suggested Hallie needed to loosen up, but he could have kept that to himself. Of all the industry events she'd attended, he hadn't once seen her with a date. She might well be the hardest-working person in this party town. After hearing how many years she'd been hustling for

Hannah, hell, Hallie deserved downtime more than any of them.

He would have liked to see her here tonight, loose and lively. He could have bought her a drink and helped coax her from her rigid shell. The idea of seducing Hallie was surprisingly appealing—regardless of the danger of becoming involved. Too bad casual flings didn't come with ironclad contracts protecting all parties when they ultimately failed.

"I'll take you up on that." Alex touched his arm with her index finger, bringing his attention back to the present.

Speaking of seduction. Apparently, his young client was working her wiles on him. He knew some a-holes in this business who would jump at the chance to bed the flirty, young brunette. He wasn't one of them. He was flattered, but he knew where to draw the line with clients. Now to turn down Alex without hurting her feelings.

Tricky.

He removed her hand from his arm and met her eyes. "There are a lot of bastards in this business, Alex. The first rule of music, hell, maybe the *only* rule, is don't offer yourself to any of them. If I had responded to you touching me with an offer of more, hopefully you would have slapped me in the face."

She blinked three times in quick succession, processing his point-blank warning. "I wasn't…"

"Oh, I know," he said to save her from embarrassment. "I just wanted to warn you about the men in this industry. Most are a quick ticket to 'Troubletown.'" She smiled at his clever use of the title of her most recent single. "As your attorney, it's my job to protect you. The world can be predatory, especially to fresh talents who haven't been in this business long." He padded the remark by adding, "Which is why I'm going to be here every step of the way to make sure you are never taken advantage of by anyone. I'm in your corner—me, and my brothers—along with Elite Records. We're your safe haven. You can count on us."

She smiled, gratitude coloring her cheeks. He might very well be the last honest lawyer on the planet, but he saw no reason to lie, cheat or steal like some of those bastards. If you were good—and Gavin was the best—there was no need to swindle anyone into doing business with you. Usually clients came to him, climbing over each other to beg for representation.

He said good-night to Alex and walked away, typing a reminder into his electronic calendar to call Brite White Tooth Powder about Alex. They needed a good ambassador. His young client was a shoo-in.

He pocketed his phone, musing how he was ten years older than Alex, but felt like he'd lived a lifetime before this one. Being the youngest of four boys, he'd often felt like he'd been playing catch-up with his older brothers. Now, each of them was either married or well on his way and he had the unique experience of *not* wanting to catch up. He had nothing against Hannah, Presley or Cassandra—they were gems—but Gavin didn't want a wife or a family. He was happy having fun on a short-term basis. He'd save the serious stuff for his career.

Like their parents, each of the Sutherland sons had

been driven to succeed. Unlike their parents, none of them had taken a shining to the family business of real estate. They'd gone into the music industry instead.

Gavin had always loved music, but couldn't sing or play a note of it. He'd been drawn to the business side, enamored by the contracts and deals.

Elite Records was pitted against rival label Cheating Hearts Records, owned by town matriarch Mags Dumond. Mags treated Beaumont Bay like one big Monopoly board, but Elite had something Cheating Hearts didn't: scruples. The Sutherland brothers prided themselves on focusing on the artist first. The strategy served them well.

As Gavin saw it, he owed his livelihood to entertainers. Without their talent, there would be no recording studios. There would be no sponsorships. There would be no benefit concerts or acoustic ballads played to small crowds on open mic night. He'd seen a lot of lawyers and agents take advantage of bright-eyed artists in Nashville and yes, here in his treasured hometown of Beaumont Bay, but Gavin's allegiance lay with his clients.

He shook a few hands and slapped some shoulders as he slowly made his way out of the party. On the elevator ride down, he recalled the seething glare Hannah had shot him before the elevator doors closed. While he was congratulating himself for so magnanimously protecting the innocent entertainers of the world, perhaps he should apologize for speaking out of turn about a close family friend.

He'd let Hannah know he hadn't meant to insult

Hallie. Explain that the booze had gone to his head, and he'd been talking out of his ass. As he stepped out of the Beaumont Hotel onto the lit street teeming with tourists and locals alike, he keyed a message into his phone to Hannah.

You know I think Hallie's great. Sorry if I acted like an ass.

There. He felt better already. He inhaled the sweet breeze of magnolias coming from the flower shop on the corner. A flash of blond hair in his periphery drew his attention. By the time he turned around, the woman had shut herself into a waiting car, its windows tinted and dark.

Evidently, his conscience thought he owed Hallie an apology, too.

Three

Early the next morning, Gavin stepped into Elite Records and greeted his brother. Will was sitting at the conference table, coffee in hand. Hannah was with him, wearing a pink pantsuit, her blond hair curled and "out to there" as Alex had described last night. Gavin still got the biggest kick out of his oldest and most serious brother finding love with a woman who sparkled from head to toe.

"Hey, Han," Gavin said as he sat down across from them.

"Hi." Her head cocked to one side, she shot him an expression he couldn't quite read. Could mean anything. She hadn't responded to his text last night. He supposed there was an outside chance she'd never received it. Before he could ask, Hallie entered the room, her mood updated to Serious 2.0.

"Gavin." Her usual businesslike tone had an edge.

Yep. Hannah had definitely shared what he'd said about Hallie at the party. He should have expected them to share everything. He also should have kept his damn thoughts to himself.

"I have the merchandising agreement for Hannah's upcoming shows in the UK. The pricing is great, and from what I can tell they're making a fair offer." Hallie handed out packets, each fastened with a gold binder clip. She then took her seat to Gavin's left—leaving one empty chair between them.

He slanted her a glance but she studiously ignored him. He turned his attention to the contract in front of him. As soon as he read the first line of the document, his personal concerns vanished. He became mesmerized by the legal speak that had once been a foreign language but was now second tongue.

He didn't find any sketchy or sneaky phrasing, but there was a clause or two he could add to the contract to ensure Hannah was a more equal partner.

His goal when negotiating was to ensure each party clocked a win. It could be a challenge to orchestrate, which he never understood. Working relationships were best when everyone was happy. The greed in this industry never failed to amaze him. It was why he charged in first and gave his full attention to his client. Contract work was often viewed as boring and tedious, but it turned him on in a way not many people understood. Gavin was his clients' biggest and best advantage.

"I'll give their office a call this afternoon." He held out his hand to take the other copies of the contracts.

"We'll have a few minor errors removed and the clause added, and you'll be set."

"Thanks, Gav." Hannah smiled prettily, relieved. Making his clients feel at ease was rewarding.

"I'll admit," Will said as he stood from the table and tossed his copy of the contract over to Gavin, "I'm smart as hell, but I don't see what you see when looking at those things."

"Practice, brother. Lots and lots of practice."

"If you'll excuse us." Will tucked his wife to his hip and sent her a heated gaze no one missed. "We have to discuss something in my office."

Then they were out, Hannah whispering something into Will's ear that Gavin was grateful he hadn't overheard. He was happy for them—he was happy for all his brothers for achieving fiancé or husband status so effortlessly—but he also did *not* need to know details.

He turned to Hallie to say what, he didn't know. How do you address someone you inadvertently insulted who refused to talk to you? "That went well."

She blinked at him.

"The contract, I mean."

She blinked again.

Oh-kay. He'd try a compliment.

"Music Keepers isn't a company I've worked with before. Good job finding them. They might be worth a second look when it comes time to re-up Cash's touring merch contract."

"Yes."

So, he'd squeezed one word out of her. At least it was an affirmative one.

"Hallie. What gives? I think I know, but I'd prefer you tell me." If he knew one thing for sure, it was that he who speaks first *loses*. If he launched into an apology for what he'd said to Hannah, he might share more than Hallie knew. And he did *not* want her to know what he'd said last night if he could avoid it.

"Why would there be something wrong?" Her hazel eyes flashed, sending an answering jolt of awareness through his chest. The idea of a feisty Hallie set him off like a rocket. It was too bad he couldn't consider her for even the briefest of flings. He'd bet he'd find passion hidden inside her if he managed to crack through her sharp exterior.

"You look different, is all," he said, shaking the thought out of his head. Her twin was his brother's wife. There was no way to have a brief *anything* with Hallie Banks—even if she didn't hate him.

She made a choking sound in the back of her throat. He sent a brief scan down her outfit. Black trousers, silky beige blouse and sensible, black high heels. Her standard office attire. Her hair was smoothed back in a smart, professional ponytail, her makeup understated and soft. When she narrowed her eyelids at him, he figured it out.

She was looking him in the eyes. Well, technically she was *glaring* at him exactly like Hannah had last night, but still. Hallie almost never met his gaze.

"I got it." He snapped his fingers. "No glasses."

Her head jerked on her neck as her eyebrows slammed down.

"You're, ah, you're not wearing glasses like you

sometimes do." Like she had nearly every time he'd seen her before. Apart from the wedding, or that time at The Cheshire when Presley had first come to town.

"Do you need me to wear them? So that you don't mistake me for Hannah?" One of those manicured eyebrows shot up and another rogue zing of awareness zapped his bloodstream.

Whoa. What the hell was *that*?

"No. Of course not."

"Are you sure?" She didn't wait for his reply, instead marching out of the conference room, her ponytail swinging behind her as she clipped down the corridor.

Well. His conversation with Hannah certainly hadn't ushered Hallie into the friend zone. She'd talked to him, though, which was a step in the right direction.

He gathered the contracts and went to his office, passing Will's closed door on the way and definitely *not* listening in case they were doing something other than business in that room. Like each other.

A few hours later, he'd successfully lost himself in work and was adding an item to his to-do list in his meticulous block lettering when a knock came at the door. "It's open."

Hannah let herself in and sat primly on the edge of the chair across from his desk, her smile both impish and knowing. Behind her hung a framed photo of her and Cash after one of their performances together. The big lights, the stage, the sweat on their brows. They were crazy talented. As proud as he was of both of them, he had never wanted fame for himself. He didn't need adoring fans. Just happy clients.

"I was going to bring this up earlier, but then Hallie came in and I figured it would be more awkward if I did."

"You told her." He leaned back in his chair and tossed his pen on top of his journal.

Hannah pulled out her cell phone and read aloud, *"You know I think Hallie's great. Sorry if I acted like an ass.'"*

"I know what it says, Han. I wrote it."

"Yes, but what the hell does it mean?" Her eyebrows winged upward. "When were you an ass, *specifically*?"

"Last night. At The Cheshire." As he spoke those words, he recalled Hannah's flashing eyes and pointed glare…and the eerie way it mirrored Hallie's reaction to him this morning. An unpleasant sensation slithered down his spine.

"I wasn't at The Cheshire last night. Will and I were at your parents' house picking up a quilt your mom sewed for us."

"Oh?"

"Yeah. I had no idea how to respond to you. I thought maybe you texted the wrong person, or you were drunk or something."

"I wish," he muttered, coming to a conclusion that had taken its sweet time getting here. He'd been cataloging the subtle differences between Hannah and Hallie for months, but apparently not in the conscious part of his brain—which would have been damn helpful *last night*.

The glasses were an obvious difference, but Hallie hadn't been wearing them today and he still couldn't have mistaken her for Hannah. There was a slight difference in their eye color—both of them had hazel eyes, but Hallie's irises held flashes of gold. Specifically, when she was angry. Like she was this morning…and *when he'd mistaken her for Hannah last night*.

No. No friggin' way. He'd addressed her as Hannah and she hadn't corrected him. Why would Hallie pretend to be her sister?

"Can you raise one eyebrow?" he blurted out. The woman under the stars at The Cheshire had done just that. He recalled the moment very clearly. He'd thought it was cute, and immediately dismissed the thought. Admiring his brother's wife was poor form—especially if Will caught wind of it.

Hannah wiggled both eyebrows in a futile attempt to force one higher than the other. "Never could. Hallie can. She does it without trying."

"Shit." He'd felt the slightest hesitation when he'd said hello to "Hannah" last night. He should've never ignored his gut.

"I'm going to go out on a limb here and assume you mistook Hallie for me?" Hannah gave him a dazzling grin, clearly enjoying this much more than he was.

He scratched his eyebrow. "That would appear to be the case."

"You were bamboozled, my friend. Out of curiosity, what did you say to Hallie, *about Hallie*?"

"Nothing I would have said to her directly, but it wasn't bad. I think she took it that way, though."

Hannah glanced at the text on her phone. "I think it's nice that you like her."

"Of course I like her." He frowned. Why wouldn't

he? "She doesn't like *me*. Especially after I implied she couldn't find a date because she works too much."

Hannah sucked in air through perfectly straight teeth. Looking at the other twin, it was impossible not to notice that the blond in her hair was much lighter than Hallie's honeyed locks. How could he have been so clueless?

Then his embarrassment faded into a more volatile emotion and he growled, "Do you two get off on pretending to be each other?" He stood and yanked his jacket from the back of his chair before palming his journal. "I recall Will having a similar issue with the two of you."

"Don't raise your voice at my wife." Will appeared out of nowhere to scowl at Gavin from the doorway.

"Oh, stop it." Hannah shoved her husband before joining him in the hall. "Gavin's just mad at himself." She addressed Gavin next. "Talk to her. Sounds like you both have some explaining to do." Hannah was still smiling.

Gavin ignored his oldest brother's fierce expression. Outside, he pulled out his phone and sent a text—to Hallie this time.

We need to talk.

He didn't expect to hear back, but he wasn't waiting around for her approval. He climbed into his stone-gray Ford F-150 truck and sped toward her apartment.

"Ready or not, Hallie Banks," he said as he gunned the engine and accelerated down the road, "here I come."

Four

Hallie parked in front of her half of the rented du-
plex, her very late take-out lunch on the passenger seat.
She'd had a busy day after she left the studio. As she
ran errands and took phone calls, Gavin's words from
last night—and his slimy attempt to worm his way out
of saying them this morning—loomed in the back of
her mind.

After the party, she'd come home and plucked the
bobby pins from her carefully coiffed hair. She'd scrubbed
off her makeup and hung the plum-colored dress on the
colorful side of her closet. Then she'd changed into a
gray shorts set and pulled out the notebook where she'd
written her checklist for the new year.

She'd grabbed a fat black marker and crossed out
Gavin's name. Honestly, she was far less angry with him

than she was with herself. This morning she'd woken feeling more charitable to herself. After a long couple of hours at the party, she'd been too tired to be witty. That was understandable. She certainly wasn't *afraid* of Gavin Sutherland. And she wasn't about to play nice when he'd insulted her to her face.

She fruitlessly tried to unlock her front door while juggling the take-out bag, her purse, a large iced tea and her briefcase when a large truck pulled into the driveway. Gavin stepped out of it, long and lean and looking like a million dollars in a suit that probably cost close to that. His tie was royal blue, his hair arranged in perfect, dark waves. His shoes were shiny and stylish. He'd be so much easier to hate if he wasn't so damn good-looking.

He didn't waste time taking her keys from her hand and opening her door for her. He stepped aside to let her go in ahead of him, but then followed her anyway, shutting them into her apartment before she could invite him.

"Won't you come in," she muttered as she plopped everything in her hands onto the kitchen table.

He dropped her keys into her purse and then stood, arms folded, and stared at her.

"What are you doing here?" she asked when it was evident he wasn't going to speak first.

"I texted you."

Yeah, well, she'd turned on the Do Not Disturb setting for his phone number so she wouldn't have to deal with him today. Perhaps a juvenile response, but he *was* disturbing.

"About what?" she asked as she pulled containers from her to-go bag.

"We need to talk." His tone was both authoritative and grave.

"No, we don't." She'd heard quite enough of what he'd had to say last night. "I'm going to eat my lunch. You can see yourself out."

Being angry with him was much easier than stepping out of her comfort zone. She popped the lid off her poke bowl and tore the paper holding a pair of wooden chopsticks.

"That was you at The Cheshire. You let me think you were Hannah."

"Yes." She paused, a chunk of raw tuna inches from her mouth. "And what an enlightening experience that was."

He leaned over her, his palms flat on her kitchen table. He looked good, but he smelled better. A hint of spice rolled off his neck, making her hungry for more than sushi.

"What is it you think you heard me say?"

Ha! What a lawyer-y question.

"I *know* what I heard." She abandoned her lunch to fold her arms over her chest. "I can't get a date. You said so yourself."

"I asked if you had one."

"You asked if I'd *landed* one."

He nodded, letting her have that, but he didn't seem happy about it. "I wasn't implying you couldn't."

"I'm not incapable of being social," she found herself

defending. "I'd been social for hours by the time you said hello. You caught me at a bad time."

He straightened and threw his arms out. "I didn't say you were incapable of being social."

"You said Hannah was the social butterfly, and I work all the time." Her voice cracked, emotion causing her throat to tighten. She was trying *not* to sound weak or defensive, but it was hard when the guy she liked way too much thought she was an antisocial stick-in-the-mud.

Rather than lean this time, he pulled out a chair and scooted closer to her. She gazed into his fathomless gray-blue eyes and briefly imagined another scenario that would bring him this close—one where they weren't arguing about her being a workaholic. One that would give her a taste of the lips she'd been longing for over the last year.

Dammit. Why hadn't she corrected him at the party? Then he would have been polite and nice and she could have been spared his uninvited opinions.

"I was complimenting your work ethic," he said. "Granted, I could have done a better job."

"Ya think?"

His mouth slipped into a smirk and his voice came out more tender than before. "I was suggesting you deserved some time off, not accusing you of not knowing how to have fun."

Well. That was sort of nice. But…

"You weren't exactly trotting out the compliments." She took a drink of her iced tea. A big enough gulp that she nearly choked when he continued.

"You want compliments? The truth is I have never been able to understand why you don't bring a date. Look at you." He did then, raking his eyes over her in a slow perusal that made her wiggle in her chair. "You're damn gorgeous. And smart. Funny. Unique."

"So *unique* you assumed I was Hannah when you saw me?" she clipped.

"Can I add smart-ass to the list?" He gave her a full-on grin, his eyes twinkling, and she suddenly regretted crossing his name out with permanent marker. Similarly, she couldn't erase her memories of what he'd said last night.

"In my defense," he continued, "I had second thoughts the moment I addressed you as Hannah. What was I supposed to do? Call you a liar? Or worse, compliment you on your smoking hot dress and ask you to dance?"

Oh, that would have been lovely.

"And then," he said, his voice low and seductive, "when I gave in to the urge to run my fingers over those creamy, exposed shoulders…"

Hallie leaned closer, hooked on his every word. He'd thought her dress was smoking hot? And he'd wanted to dance with her? To *touch* her?

"Would you have come to my funeral?" he murmured.

She blinked. "What?"

"If you had actually been Hannah, Will would have murdered me."

"You're saying it's my fault," she grumbled, feeling regret tenfold.

"Partially. I'm sorry if I offended you. I recognize when someone needs a break, and you, Hallie, have earned one." He took a deep breath before he continued, "I was raised in a family whose motto is work hard and work harder. I've resisted that with everything I am. Everyone has a breaking point, you know."

"And you think I'm at a breaking point?"

"Not yet." His smile was soft, his eyes locked on hers.

She was still in shock. She assumed he could take her or leave her and that she was alone in admiring him from afar. Now he was smirking and smiling and saying sexy things to her. It was too much to process over a tuna poke bowl.

"Forgive me?" He offered his hand and she regarded it dubiously. She didn't recall ever shaking Gavin's hand. Even when they'd first met. Overwhelmed by the need to touch him, she agreed without a second thought and slid her hand into his.

"There's nothing to forgive." She was going to add a thank-you for the compliments and a return apology for faking her identity, but the words frittered into the sizzling air between them.

His hand was larger than hers, his skin slightly tanned. He had long fingers and attractive knuckles. His grip was firm, yet gentle. And warm. So warm. His smile held, his eyelids sinking to half-mast.

"Hallie Banks. Golden eyes, dimples, able to lift one eyebrow without trying. Mistaking you for your sister isn't something you'll be able to accuse me of again."

She was so smitten by his presence, his unwavering eye contact and the feel of his skin against hers, she didn't let go right away when he tried to take his hand back. Her uttered apology was a mere whisper, lost under his husky laugh.

"Glad we cleared that up. I'll let you eat." He patted the table twice and stood. Her insides jumped, urging her to walk with him to the door, but in the end she stayed rooted to her seat, unable to rise to the occasion.

Yet again.

Hallie met Presley at Rise and Grind every week. Sometimes they enjoyed scones on Sunday or sipped tea on Tuesday. Today was Flat White Friday.

The appointment had been on her calendar for a week, but since Hallie hadn't shaken off the run-in with Gavin at her apartment, she'd been tempted to cancel. Reason being, she knew she'd want to tell Presley everything, and since Pres was engaged to Gavin's brother Cash, Hallie probably shouldn't.

Presley smoothed her red hair behind her ear, her engagement ring glinting in the sunshine streaming in through the windows of the café. Cash had proposed onstage to his lovely bride-to-be over the summer. Presley had moved from Florida to Tennessee right away. Since then, she and Hallie had spent a lot of time together and had become close friends in a relatively short period of time.

Coffee cup halfway to her lips, Presley asked, "So what's new with you?" and Hallie nixed the idea of keeping quiet about Gavin. She expelled the entire story, sharing the details of what happened at The Cheshire

Sunday night and Elite Records on Monday morning, and finished off with how he had barged into her house that afternoon. She left out the part where he'd flattered her half to death.

"Like he has any room to tell you what to do with your free time?" Presley exploded, drawing attention from a neighboring table. "Who cares if you dated a thousand men a week or zero? It's none of his business." She took a long sip from her cup and her ire faded into a warm smile. "Mmm. I love Flat White Friday."

Hallie chuckled, feeling better having told someone. Hannah had asked, but all Hallie had admitted was that she hadn't wanted to embarrass Gavin, so she hadn't corrected his error. Granted, Hannah had not believed her, but at least she didn't ask any more questions.

"Well, he did apologize," Hallie told Pres. "And then he said he didn't mean it the way it sounded. He also said I deserve a break, and pointed out how his family is rife with workaholics."

"Too true. I hear Cash strumming his guitar in the wee hours some nights and then, like clockwork, he's out on the dock at sunrise strumming some more." Presley's smile was fond. "I love his passion."

Hallie was certain her friend loved more than Cash's passion for music. It'd been a long road for them. They'd briefly dated in college before he'd returned home to Beaumont Bay and left Presley in Florida. When she came here to interview him this past summer, they realized their feelings for each other hadn't gone anywhere, despite the years and miles that had kept them apart.

It was so sweet Hallie could puke.

"So after he told you to take a break, what happened?" Presley pushed.

"Nothing happened. I mean, he shook my hand and said...um..." Hallie was suddenly self-conscious. Gavin's compliments might as well have been rated X for the images they'd put in her head. She hadn't yet reconciled his "creamy shoulders" comment. What was she supposed to do with *that*? "Never mind."

"Uh-huh. No. You have to tell me now."

"It's nothing, really. Do you want a scone? I want a scone." Before she could stand, Pres grabbed her wrist. Hallie lowered into her seat. Knowing she'd lose the battle with her headstrong friend, she said, "He told me I was gorgeous and he said he couldn't understand why I showed up single everywhere."

Her friend's expression melted a microsecond before she said, "That's sort of sweet."

"It sort of was."

"You *are* gorgeous."

"I look like Hannah," Hallie mumbled automatically.

"You look exactly like Hannah," her friend confirmed. "Hannah also looks exactly like you. I can't imagine how difficult it would be to find your own identity when you have a duplicate copy, but Hallie, you have to know that you two stand apart from each other."

"Do we?"

"When you're not pretending to be her, yes," Presley said with a kind smile.

Hallie sagged in her seat. "Ugh. He makes me so nervous!" She couldn't imagine what would happen the next time she saw him. Now that he'd touched her and mentioned her shoulders. Now that she knew what it was like to be under his unwavering attention.

"Because you find him hot, which he is."

"Yeah." Hallie didn't bother to deny that glaringly obvious fact.

"Sounds like he finds you hot, too."

"He pointed out mine and Hannah's physical differences and vowed to never make the mistake of mixing us up again."

"The dimples," Presley listed. "Glasses, clothing styles."

"Yeah, those. He also noticed I can lift one eyebrow. Hannah can't. And my eyes are slightly more golden than hers."

"They are?" Presley squinted at her. "Oh my God, you're right. I never noticed." Then she sang, "But Gavin *diiiid.*"

"Shh. We're in public."

Palming her coffee cup, Pres crossed one arm over her middle. Her next suggestion bottomed out Hallie's stomach. "If I were you, I'd tell him if he's so great at relaxing, he should give you a tutorial."

Hallie laughed. "Yeah, sure."

Presley didn't crack a smile. "I'm serious. You're not a workaholic, Hallie, but you could stand to have a little fun. Gavin is fun. He's also a nice guy you can trust. I mean, hello, you know his whole family."

Yes, and that bit made her nervous, too. Like they'd look at her and Gavin and wonder what on earth he saw in her. But that couldn't be the case, could it? Presley clearly thought this was a good idea.

"He's attractive and he finds you attractive. Ask him to show you a good time. Live a little. You've earned it."

Following her slightly alarming suggestion, Presley decided she wanted scones after all and excused herself to the counter. Hallie watched out the window as people strode by on the sidewalk, her mind on—who else?—Gavin Sutherland.

There was no doubt he could teach her a thing or two about having fun. He was the consummate playboy. Charm came second nature to him—maybe first. She'd been convincing herself they were opposites for months, but… What if she could use that to her benefit? What if she bent her rules and allowed him to help her climb out of her shell?

It wasn't such a crazy idea when she thought about it.

Hannah had been encouraging Hallie to loosen up for years. Heck, Hannah had been the one to pack half of Hallie's closet with couture gowns and sequined high heels. Her experiment hadn't gone totally awry. Hallie had felt pretty the night at The Cheshire. Before she'd worn the plum-colored gown, black and beige had been the only two shades on her color wheel.

Hallie had been the serious, studious sister for far too long. She'd been holding everything together—her sister's future, her own business—for so long, she'd nearly forgotten how to have fun. And whenever she broke one of her so-called "rules," she promptly beat herself up over it. Recent incident included.

No more.

Presley was right. Hallie *could* stand to have some fun. And Gavin happened to be capable of walking the tightrope-thin line between work and play while wearing a blindfold.

She smiled, the idea exciting and new. What if Hallie could be fresh and fun? Light and lovable? All she had to do was convince Gavin to help her let her hair down, and in return, she could...um. Well, he had to want something from her, right?

But *what*?

Five

In Will and Hannah's living room, Hallie was bent over her laptop finalizing her sister's itinerary.

Hannah swept into the room with yet another piece of Louis Vuitton luggage and added it to the pile. She and Will were off to France, a working vacation since Hannah would be performing at a special charity event there.

Hallie thought of how Gavin had said his family was full of workaholics and smiled. She could slot herself and Hannah under that column, too.

No sooner than she thought of him, her sister said, "Oh, good. Gavin made it."

"What? Why?" Hallie plucked her glasses off her nose and reached for her hair, which was currently in a sloppy twist at the back of her head and—*fantastic*—there was a pencil stuck in there, too.

"What are you fretting about? He accepted your apology." Hannah's eyes sparkled when she added, "Besides, I have a text proving he thinks you're *great*."

"Stop," Hallie mouthed as her sister pulled open the front door.

"Signed, sealed and now delivered," Gavin announced.

Hannah took the envelope from his hand and thanked him, but instead of ushering him on his way, she invited him in with a, "Do you want a cup of coffee?"

"No, thanks. I—" But then his eyes skated over to where Hallie stood and he grinned. "Actually, yes. I was going to stop at Rise and Grind, but since you offered."

"Perfect. Help yourself. You know where everything is." Hannah held the door open for Will, who was toting more designer luggage.

"Is this the last of it?" he asked before greeting his brother with a "Hey, Gav" on his way out.

"Yes, that's it. We can go. I have everything. You good, Hallie?"

"Uh—" Was it noon already? And was Hannah really sticking her here with Gavin? Alone?! Once again, the bravado she'd felt failed her when the object of her infatuation was standing in the same room.

"Lock up for me. I'll send you photos of the Eiffel Tower." Hannah hugged her, giving her an extra-hard squeeze. She must've sensed Hallie's alarm, because next she whispered, "Enjoy your company."

Hallie gave her sister a warning glare. "Be safe."

"I've got her." Will's warm gaze landed on his wife.

Hannah was in the best hands, which helped Hallie relax some about sending her sister over the big blue ocean without her. Will and Hannah gathered the rest of the bags and Hallie shut the door behind them.

"Can I make you one?" Gavin offered, pouring creamer into a coffee mug.

"No, thanks. I'm wired as it is." God knew what she'd say to him if she drank more caffeine. She forced herself to sit, and then turned her focus to the laptop in front of her. She hadn't expected to see him this soon, and as a result she wasn't ready to execute the decision she'd made two days ago at the café. She wasn't good at winging it. Life required planning. As much as possible.

He settled on the couch next to her, leaving little space between them. His piney, spicy scent surrounded her and she had to fight the urge to lean in and inhale deeply.

"What's on the docket today for you?" he asked, easing back on the couch and crossing one leg ankle-to-knee.

"Oh, you know. A million things." She gestured at the screen nervously, wishing he'd have sat in the chair across from her instead of beside her. She could barely think with him this close.

"Why am I not surprised," he murmured.

"What's that supposed to mean?" she snapped.

He paused, the mug almost touching his lips. His perfect lips fringed with the perfect amount of facial scruff. Why did he have to be so damn attractive? It was irritating. "Nothing. You're not still upset with me are you? I thought we agreed that was behind us."

Right. Shoot. She was overreacting. He'd made her feel more than a little self-conscious since he'd said she was no fun and worked all the time. Especially since she continued proving his point time and again.

"Yes." It was a strange response, but she didn't dare try to form a complete sentence. Not while he was infiltrating her personal space. She could almost feel the hum of awareness between them—or at least stringing from her to him. Which meant she really should attempt to speak so he wouldn't think she was a tongue-tied twit. "Um. Are you—what are you doing today?"

There. That sounded normal.

A slow smile spread his lips. Her mind blanked. He was too gorgeous. Especially in a navy blue suit and pastel pink tie. His messy hair tempted her to run her fingers through it.

"You want the truth?"

She nodded, unsure.

He set his mug on the glass coffee table and then let out a sigh. "I'm in purgatory, Hals."

She felt her eyebrow lift and waited for him to explain.

"You know I built the house on the lake, right?"

Boy, did she. She'd been dying to see it after overhearing him, or Will, or Cash, or Hannah talking about it. From what she'd heard, Gavin's new-build was more of a mansion. It was located between the main lake and a smaller, private one, which meant not one but *two* amazing views. With the leaves changing color, those views were probably nothing short of paradise.

"Yes."

"Another yes. We're two for two." His grin remained and she jerked her attention to his casually folded hands, once again admiring his fingers. There was no safe space to rest her eyes on him. "One would assume after making approximately two *million* decisions during the building of a new house, I'd be done. Evidently, I have to make two million more decisions about the interior."

His smile faltered, giving way to a new expression. He appeared well and truly miffed.

"My interior designer is amazing. Adore her. She's smart, she's savvy. She's expensive, but worth every dime." His gray-blue eyes held Hallie's for the count of three and she had to fight a blush. "Anyway. The big stuff's already moved in, but a lot of rooms need attention. I don't care about wall hangings or curtains or rugs. Ruby is doing her job and doing it well. Says she needs to 'nail down my style.'" He capped the sentence with air quotes. "I've been avoiding her for two weeks, but today I agreed to let her come over and torture me."

Hallie couldn't help it. She laughed. "You poor thing. Forced to pick designer furnishings for your zillion-dollar mansion on the lake."

"Lakes," he corrected.

"Right. Lakes."

"I'd do anything to get out of it. Who the hell knows how to sum up their style in a few words anyway? I've never thought about it. I'm a bachelor. I'm clueless."

"You seem to dress yourself okay."

"Stylist." He held out the side of his jacket and showed off the button-down shirt beneath it. She didn't think she'd ever been distracted by a flash of a pectoral muscle behind 100 percent cotton before, but her mind was suddenly scrambled.

"Someone else may have styled your suit, but you wear it well. Like you belong in it."

His shoulders straightened at the compliment. "Go on."

She was unsuccessful at smothering her next smile. The air between them had shifted, albeit unexpectedly. Instead of a whirlwind of choking awareness kicking up dust and debris, the vibe between them was friendly. Almost…easy. "A house is the same as clothing. You try on a few things to see if they fit and if it feels good, you know."

Now he looked confused.

She licked her lips and tried again. "Clearly you're not afraid of color." She gestured to his suit. "And your style, while simple, is pristine." She touched her finger to the pocket square nestled in his suit jacket. "Everything in its place."

His eyes followed the movement of her hand as she pulled it back into her lap. The friendly vibe shifted yet again, to a crackling tension that wasn't the least bit unpleasant.

"Anyway." She cleared her throat. "There's never a speck of lint on your jacket."

"Never?" he murmured almost seductively. How did he do that? Make an innocuous word sound like pure sex?

"Uh, from…from what I've noticed."

"Hmm. I didn't realize you'd noticed."

She let out a nervous laugh.

His eyes dashed to his folded hands and he sighed.

"If I had someone like you to help me out, this wouldn't be such a miserable task." He reclaimed his coffee mug.

She was about to dismissively agree when she realized he'd revealed exactly what he needed from her. Maybe if she offered to take some decision-making off his plate with his interior designer, he'd consider helping Hallie learn how to have more fun. And with Hannah out of the country for a little while, it was the perfect time for Hallie to step out from behind her older sister's shadow. Not that Hannah wouldn't approve, but in case she didn't… Hallie didn't want to hear about it.

"I—there was actually something I wanted to ask you." She swallowed, her throat suddenly dry. "A favor."

"Oh, yeah?" He leaned closer to her, dropping his elbows to his knees while cradling his mug.

"Yes." She blew out her next breath through pursed lips and admitted, "But I'm almost too nervous to ask."

Ten different scenarios flitted through Gavin's head, and every last one of them involved Hallie with her lips on part of his body.

Any part. He wasn't picky.

As much lecturing as he'd given himself recently about why he shouldn't seduce Hallie Banks—the messy family ties, her apparent distaste for him—he'd changed his mind since sitting beside her on this couch.

She'd been peeking from under her lashes at him, sending him nervous smiles. She'd touched his pocket square. Not typically a flirty move, but for Hallie it kind of was. She went out of her way to avoid him normally and here she was casually touching him *and* had a favor to ask?

Sign him up.

He couldn't help hoping she was girding her loins to ask a favor of him of a sexual variety. Hell, he'd settle for the *sensual* variety. He wasn't seeing anyone at the moment. Even if he was, he would have had to end it since his thoughts were consumed by the blonde sitting next to him.

"It's more of a proposition," Hallie went on.

Hell, *yes*. He set his mug down and rubbed his hands together in anticipation. "Okay. Hit me."

When her pink tongue shot out to wet her bottom lip, he was pulled toward her as if by a tractor beam. Halfway between scooting closer and offering his mouth as tribute, she spoke...and said the opposite of what he'd been hoping she would say.

"You were right." She reached over and shut her laptop. "When you said I work too much."

He flinched. Not this again.

"I'm not interested in rehashing the argument. I'm wondering if you'd be willing to teach me what you know about breaking rules."

"Breaking...rules?" His first thought was that she was in some sort of legal trouble. That she'd gotten into a scrape with a big company with bigger lawyers. Or maybe she was considering a gray area lingering between legal and illegal activities and needed his advice about navigating it. "Hallie, if you're asking me to represent you, we need to proceed very carefully. I can't advise you to break the law, even if—"

"No! No, nothing like that." She shook her head and a tendril of blond hair sneaked out and brushed the side of her mouth. She tucked it behind her ear and it sprang out again.

"Okay. Then what?" Without thinking, he smoothed the lock behind her ear again, watching as her mouth dropped open softly. She really was beautiful. And so different from Hannah. This close to her he couldn't overlook their subtle differences. Each of Hallie's features was far more appealing to him than her sister's.

"Um." She closed her eyes like she was rerouting her thoughts. A reaction to him touching her, he'd bet. "I want to have more fun in my personal life. I don't go out much, unless the event is a write-off. And I guess… I'm having trouble knowing how." Her cheeks pinked further.

He steadily held her gaze, granting her the time to finish her thought. He was intrigued as hell. Teaching Hallie Banks to break some rules wasn't so much a favor for her as it was a gift for him.

"My whole life," she started quietly, "I've watched Hannah take big risks. I want to try. And I figured, since you made having fun part of your credo—"

"I have a credo?"

"—you could teach me how." She held up one finger. "Safely. I don't want to skydive or climb a mountain. Or do anything that would risk my reputation with my new client."

"You have a new client?" Color him impressed. She'd recently decided to expand her roster beyond her twin sister's career, and she'd landed someone already.

"Martina Merriweather, Bernie's daughter." Her

gaze flicked away when she said, "I met him at The Cheshire."

"So, Hallie Banks appeared to a lucky few that night." When she bit her lip, he placed his hand over hers and gave her fingers a gentle squeeze. "Great job. She's lucky to have you."

Her grin was proud. "Thank you."

"You're welcome."

"I'm not asking for charity from you, though," she said, suddenly serious. "I want to give you something in return."

"I'm all ears." And other body parts, too, but he refrained from mentioning them.

"I'll agree to be the go-between for you and the interior decorator."

He frowned. "I'm sorry?"

"You might not have any idea what kind of furniture or rugs or window treatments to choose for your house, but I do. I saw your minimalist condominium once—"

"You did?"

She quirked her lips. "Yes. I stopped by with Hannah and Will."

Had he not noticed? Or had she made herself as small as possible so he wouldn't?

"Anyway, your place was nice, but barren. I heard Hannah say your new house has a separate office for clients, so you'll want to make a good impression. And being someone who understands both decor and the music industry…"

"You know what I need." His voice was gravel. She hadn't offered to kiss him senseless, but his brain hadn't received the memo yet. "Are you sure you're up to the task of answering questions involving rug pile height and whatever the hell wainscoting is?"

Hallie pointed to a wall with decorative paneling covering the bottom half. "That's wainscoting. So, yes."

Well. His day just became a hell of a lot more interesting. Helping Hallie have fun would not only satisfy his fresh curiosity about her, but it also held the added bonus of ending his decorator headaches.

"Very well. I accept your offer. I'll show you how to break the rules in exchange for your expertise with Ruby."

"*Safely* break the rules," she amended.

"Safely," he agreed. He would have done it for no trade at all, but if she needed to feel as if she was contributing, he could use her help. Not much in life made him wilt, but evaluating the subtle differences between cream, eggshell and off-white had weakened him like a recently shorn Sampson. "When do you want to start?"

"As soon as possible." As if worried she sounded overeager, she quickly added, "If that's okay?"

"How about now?" His mind on kissing her, he lifted his hand with the intent of cupping her jaw and tasting those lips. She misunderstood and thrust her hand into his, giving it a firm shake.

"Thank you. You won't be disappointed." She chewed on the plush bottom lip he wished he was kissing. "At the risk of sounding like the workaholic you accused me of being, there's no way I can meet with Ruby today. I have an appointment in an hour."

"No problem." And it wasn't a problem, not really.

He could bide his time. Where Hallie was concerned, he'd been around her plenty without acting on a single one of his impulses. Impulses he'd fervently ignored until now. Part of his change of heart was thanks to Will and Hannah leaving town. He wondered if their absence had similarly fueled Hallie's request. "Leave it to me, Hals. I'll show you how to have fun."

As much as she could stand to have with him.

Six

After a client meeting, Gavin was walking along one of the main drags downtown when he spotted two women he knew very well. One of them had red hair that appeared fiery in the autumn sunshine.

"Well, if it isn't none other than Presley Cole."

Gavin had known Pres for years—prior to her engagement to his brother. He found her fun and refreshing—the perfect foil for Cash, who had been far too self-sacrificial before she reentered his life.

The woman walking with her fluttered her eyelashes, a demure smile on her face.

"It's Hallie, right?" he teased, pleased when one corner of her mouth lifted.

"Very funny." Hallie rolled her eyes.

"I thought so." He was looking forward to being

around her a lot more than usual given their recently solidified "rule breaking" deal.

"What brings you to our neck of the woods, Gavin?" Presley, a to-go cup of coffee in hand, asked.

"I was visiting a client, and, hate to break it to you, but this is not *your* neck of the woods, Tallahassee. You only recently moved here."

"I'm nearly a Sutherland." She wiggled her fingers at him, showing off her engagement ring.

"What are you two up to?" he asked. Hallie seemed shier than yesterday. He was looking forward to having her to himself again, and as soon as possible.

"We were just wrapping up," Presley chirped. "I promised Cash I would meet him." She looked at Hallie, whose eyes widened slightly. "I totally forgot to tell you. Darn. I'm sure Gavin would give you a ride home."

He slanted a glance at Presley, who wobbled her head in an enthusiastic nod. He saw what was going on here.

"Ah, no problem. I have to run an errand, so you'd have to come with." He tilted his head at Hallie, who seemed thoroughly inconvenienced and maybe a little pissed off. It was a good look on her. It sparked the gold in her eyes and flushed her cheeks.

"I didn't realize I was such a *burden*," she told Presley. Yep, pissed off.

"Definitely not a burden," he assured her. "Since you agreed to help me with my interior designer, maybe you could help me out with where I'm going today, too." He nodded at his Ford truck, parked across the street. "I'm trading her in today. The lease is up, and I could use a second opinion. If you don't mind, of course."

"Yes, Hallie mentioned your *agreement*." Presley glanced at her friend meaningfully. "This is an opportunity for spontaneity."

Hallie pursed her lips.

"Have fun!" Pres scooped Hallie into a quick hug, slapped Gavin on the arm and jogged to her car as fast as her high-heeled sandals would carry her.

Hallie crossed her arms over her chest. "You don't have to take me with you. I can call a car."

"Why would you do that when I have a perfectly good truck?"

"That you're about to trade in."

He shrugged. "Life is for living, Hals."

Her eyes sparked again, but this time it wasn't caused by anger or nerves. If he wasn't mistaken, she liked the nickname. He'd never heard anyone call her anything other than Hallie. He'd consider her first rule well and truly broken.

At the dealership, Gavin waved to his friend Chad, who was racing across the showroom floor to meet him. Chad liked Gavin, probably because the youngest Sutherland had a bad habit of trading in his cars on a regular basis. Or a *good* habit, depending on which one of them you asked.

"Mr. Sutherland. I have the perfect truck picked out for you. And a couple of other contenders, as well. I know how you like options."

Gavin stuck his hands in his pockets. "Actually, I want to look at something sporty today. Fast. *Fun.* In sleek silver or cherry red. I wouldn't be opposed to royal blue, though it's not my first choice."

"No problem." Chad smiled over at Hallie and, being the good guy he was, offered his hand. "Chad King. And I know who you are. Hannah Banks. Legendary superstar."

Well, crap. No good deed went unpunished.

"Actually, this is Hannah's twin sister, Hallie— Hannah's manager."

"I'm so sorry." Chad looked chagrined for a second before saying, "You two look exactly alike. *Exactly.*"

Hallie pulled her hand from Chad's and waved off the apology. "Don't worry about it. You wouldn't believe how often it happens. Even with people we've known for *years*." She dragged out the word *years* and slid a feisty glance over at Gavin when she did it.

Wasn't she *so* funny.

"Same price range as the trucks?" Chad asked Gavin.

"No limit. Show us the best you have. I'm feeling spendy today."

Chad's eyes popped with excitement before he scampered off, promising to return with keys. Gavin turned to Hallie, expecting to see excitement on her pretty face. Instead, she regarded him sternly.

"Do you know how much money you waste by leasing? Buying is the more financially sound decision. And if you were smart you would drive a used car rather than new, which loses thirty percent of its value the moment you drive it off the lot."

"I feel like you misunderstood me when I extended this invitation. I wanted your advice on style, not price. Besides, it's no fun to drive a used car."

"There's more to life than fun—" She paused, her mouth hanging open for a beat before she bit her lip.

"A belief we're going to work on changing for you today." He offered his hand. "Come with me."

She hesitated for a beat before slipping her hand into his. He guided her through the showroom to stand in front of a tricked-out, completely impractical, bumblebee yellow sports car. His mouth over her ear, he murmured, "Driving this beauty off the showroom floor without haggling over price—now *that's* fun."

She peered at him through her eyelashes, the edge of her smile appearing and giving him a preview of one delicious dimple. He couldn't help admiring her full mouth, or leaning closer. Unfortunately, Chad showed up at that moment and ushered them outside.

Hallie didn't know what Gavin was up to, but she had to admit picking out an incredibly expensive, indulgent and, yes, *fun* sports car was the highlight of her day.

Of course, that could be partly because he'd not only been standing very close to her since they arrived at the dealership, but was also holding her hand as they admired a sleek red sports car.

"The color's Candied Apple," Chad said when Hallie touched the gleaming hood. "Excellent choice. Want to take her for a spin?"

"Yes." Gavin smiled down at her. "We would."

Chad opened the passenger-side door for her and then rounded to the driver's side. Gavin lowered onto the leather seat and gripped the wheel with both hands.

After a brief tutorial from Chad, the salesman waved them off.

"We'll have her back within the hour," Gavin said.

Chad patted the top of the car. "Take your time." Then he jogged across the parking lot to greet his next customer.

"Is it the Sutherland name that beckons this sort of VIP treatment?" Hallie ran her hand over the leather dashboard. It really was a beautiful car, and she'd never been much of a car girl.

"It could be, but in Chad's case, I think it's mostly gratitude for keeping him from getting the hell beat out of him in high school." Gavin put the car into gear and rolled out of the parking lot, navigating into the busy afternoon traffic.

"You protected him?"

"You sound surprised. You don't think I could? He and I might be roughly the same size now, but he was a skinny fifteen-year-old."

She had to laugh at Gavin's cockiness. Chad was passably attractive and basically the same size as Gavin, but the car salesman didn't have the fantastic jawline or scruff Gavin had. Chad was wider in the shoulders with a touch of a belly at his belt line, whereas Gavin was as sleek and muscular as a jungle cat. She'd had the privilege of noting his rippling muscles whenever he'd been shirtless on the boat. He worked hard on his body. She'd seen the evidence whenever he arrived at the studio after a run, sweat sparkling on his brow.

Sort of like the sweat on her own brow now. She

swiped it away and turned her thoughts from Gavin—clothed or unclothed.

"I'm not surprised," she said. "Protecting people is what you do. Though nowadays from more than losing their lunch money."

He glanced away from the road long enough to send her a warm smile. Like the compliment had touched him. But that couldn't have been a revelation. He had to know he was a good person.

She'd always admired his laid-back style. He wasn't pushy, but he was firm. He was likable, funny, and his clients trusted him without exception. Hannah hadn't hesitated to work with him after she and Will were together. And Presley had been singing Gavin's praises for as long as Hallie had known her. No way could Gavin have missed the hero worship coming at him from all sides.

She focused out the windshield as the next turn took them away from busy traffic and toward proper country territory. Beaumont Bay was a bustling, wealthy, busy city, but there was still plenty of undeveloped, untouched land. Mountain View Lake and the trees beyond hid numerous large houses in their hills you wouldn't notice if you weren't looking for them.

"I don't remember Chad sanctioning you to take this car off-road." Her voice vibrated as the wheels hit a particularly rough patch.

"You sound worried." His cunning grin dared her to argue.

"I'm not worried," she lied rather than explain how rocks scuffing the paint could cost him.

"Good. You and I are officially on the clock. We're going to break your first rule today."

She snapped her head around to challenge him, but he appeared deadly serious, even with a big grin on his face. She was about to ask him which rule he was referring to when he pulled over, threw the car into Park and climbed out. By the time he opened her door for her, she was shaking her head.

"Oh, no. I am not driving this car."

He offered his hand. "Yes. You are."

"Did you happen to notice the price sticker in the window behind me?"

As if he hadn't, he squinted at the sticker now. "So?"

"*So*. What if I bonk into something? Like a tree. Or…a ten-point buck?"

"You're funny." He laughed and her stomach fluttered. There weren't many men whose laugh registered in her stomach. That was Gavin's superpower. "Give me your hand. I mean it, Hals. We're not going back until you drive this baby."

What was it about the cute, shortened version of her name she liked so much? She'd always been *Hallie* growing up—unless someone was calling her Hannah— and hadn't thought much of having her own nickname. Gavin had given her one, and it felt special. Especially rolling off his amazing lips.

She slapped her palm into his, noting the firm warmth of his hand as he helped her from the car. Then he sat in the seat she'd been in, giving her no choice but to climb into the driver's seat.

Behind the wheel of the car, her heart pounded.

"You heard Chad go over the basics. Do you have any questions?"

"I don't think so." She flexed her fingers as she studied the fancy lights glowing from the dashboard. It was a gorgeous piece of machinery. And the most expensive car she'd ever sat in. She favored a more conservative ride...one that didn't cost as much as, say, a *house*.

"I want you to drive up this hill, take a right onto Magnolia Lane and then push the gas pedal down as hard as you dare." He pointed at the speedometer. "She goes up to one hundred and eighty."

As he talked, her eyes grew wider and wider. "I'm not going to speed in a car no one owns."

"Don't be ridiculous. The dealership owns it."

"You're not funny."

"You were the one who wanted to break rules. This is a baby step." His thick eyebrows lifted. "Don't back out on me now."

He was right. She had asked him to help her break her rules. Speeding down a country road was fairly tame. The idea made her uncomfortable, but wasn't that the point of this entire experiment?

"Do you know how to drive a stick?" he asked.

"Don't you think I would've admitted if I didn't?" She threw the car into gear and eased off the clutch, anticipation thrumming through her veins. "Gram taught me how to drive a stick."

"Eleanor Banks. A legend." He buckled his seat belt. "Let's go, then. I'm in your capable hands."

Seven

Hallie rested one hand on the wheel and the other on the stick shift between them. Her nails were short but manicured with a slightly transparent, shell-colored nail polish. Her clothing was professional and monochromatic yet inexplicably sexy.

He couldn't fathom why she'd decided to blend in with the woodwork when she was so damn interesting. Unpacking the parcel that was Hallie Banks was a hell of a lot more fun than he would have imagined.

She squealed as the car jerked under them, her laughter contagious. She wasn't going the speed limit, but held the wheel like she was breaking the sound barrier. This car should have shot off like a cannon considering the horsepower under the hood. She was driving like she was chauffeuring a little old lady to a salon appointment.

"How'd you decide to go into management?" he asked, genuinely curious.

Her eyebrows lifted—both of them—but she didn't take her eyes off the road. "I'm naturally organized. And Hannah is naturally talented."

"Seems like your mother or your father would've taken that on." He didn't know much about the Banks sisters' parents, only that they weren't around much.

"Mom and Dad are avid travelers. They've always been on the move. Gram raised Hannah and me from the time we were five years old. Mom and Dad call and visit as often as possible, but we never lacked for anything considering Gram had our backs."

He hadn't known any of that. He was mildly alarmed. His parents were *very* involved in their children's lives. The Sutherland sons hadn't gone into commercial real estate, but it hadn't stopped Travis and Dana Sutherland from offering unsolicited advice.

"Gram taught us how to be smart in the industry. She encouraged us to follow our hearts. Hannah had a natural love for singing and music and was always performing. I'm more of a behind-the-scenes girl."

"You're crazy smart, you mean."

She didn't deny it, but she did laugh. "You're one to talk, Mr. Music Lawyer. I can't make out half the words in the contracts I'm handed."

"That's purposeful. Lawyers make a lot of money translating for you layfolk." He was only half kidding. Most contracts were purposefully *confusing*. It just so happened he liked legal speak. He was good at it. When he realized not many people were, he saw an opening to make a damn good living.

"Well, I've always found you very impressive."

He sat a little taller. It wasn't like Hallie to compliment him, and maybe he needed the reminder more than he would've thought. Sometimes he felt lost in the sea of his brothers, with Luke manning the hottest nightspots in town, Cash being a world-renowned country music superstar and Will running a legendary recording studio in Beaumont Bay. And they weren't succeeding only professionally. Each of his brothers had landed a smart, funny, gorgeous woman and would soon start their own families. Their lots in life weren't anything Gavin had aspired to before, but he couldn't help feeling as if he was behind in a race he'd never entered.

He could totally relate to Hallie feeling as if she wasn't reaching the high bar Hannah had set.

"What took you so long to sign more clients?" he asked.

"Not all of us can be overachievers," she said, her assessment of him nearly the opposite of the one he'd just made about himself. "I wanted to make sure I wasn't shorting Hannah before I took on someone else. Taking care of clients is like taking care of children, I imagine. I don't want one of them to get less attention than the other."

Like Hallie had with Hannah? He was newly regretting mistaking her for her twin.

"That night at The Cheshire," he started.

"I should have corrected you."

"Yeah, but I was the one who jumped to the conclusion you were Hannah based on the color of your dress." But now that she'd mentioned it… "Why didn't you correct me?"

"I didn't want to embarrass you." She flexed her hands, resting at the ten o'clock and two o'clock positions on the steering wheel.

"You didn't want to embarrass me," he repeated, not buying the excuse.

"I was on my way out anyway. I didn't know you were going to launch into a tirade about me."

He dropped his head back on the seat rest. "It wasn't a tirade."

"I know. In hindsight, I needed to hear it. Presley agreed with you and told me I should consider loosening up. You're both right. I don't let myself have fun."

"Which is why you're here with me today," he said, happy to change the subject. He'd rather not revisit the moment he'd been insulting at worst, insensitive at best. They approached the very definition of a back road, its edges lined with tall grass beneath an overhang of orange-and-yellow-leaved trees. "Turn right."

She stepped on the brakes and sent a wary glance down the dirt and gravel lane. "Here?"

He didn't hesitate. "Here."

He must've said it with enough authority to convince her. She eased off the clutch and turned right. It was a nice fall day in Beaumont Bay, no rain or wind. Far off the beaten path, with little danger of oncoming cars, this was basically an abandoned road. The house sitting off to the side near the end had long ago fallen to the ground.

"On these country roads, the speed limit is fifty.

Common knowledge states you're safe from getting a ticket if you drive five over the speed limit, but as the saying goes, nine you're mine."

"So you would like me to go fifty-eight?"

"No. *I* would like you to go *eighty*-eight."

She smiled a pretty smile. For a second, he thought she might argue, but then she rolled her shoulders and palmed the gearshift. "Hold on to your butt."

She gunned the engine, accelerating until the passing landscape became a blur. The speedometer hovered at around fifty-five miles per hour. But by the gleeful look on Hallie's face, she might as well have been driving at warp speed. She let out a "woo-hoo!" followed by an effervescent laugh. Gavin couldn't help a low chuckle of his own.

She took the next curve well, pressing the gas pedal instead of the brake and sending dust into a cloud behind them. He checked the speedometer again. Fifty-seven. Not bad for her first attempt at rule breaking.

At the end of the lane, where brush was overgrown at a dead end, she eased to a stop. Her eyes were wild, her energy contagious. "That was fun."

"Told you." Racing along a dirt road behind the wheel of a $100,000 car he didn't own *was* fun, but not half as fun as watching Hallie enjoy herself.

He opened his mouth to ask if she'd like to drive back to the dealership or test her speeding skills on another road when she palmed his cheeks and kissed him.

He was so startled by the move, he barely had time to register the soft press of her lips, the gentle hum at the back of her throat. A second before his eyes would have sank closed, her pillowy mouth left his. Way, *way* too soon.

She pulled back and blinked big hazel eyes at him, her slender fingers still touching his face. He was struck stupid by her boldness. Days ago, she couldn't look at him and here she was kissing him. He only wished he'd have been more present during those few sluggish seconds where her lips had clung to his. He'd felt her kiss all the way down to the soles of his feet.

If a tepid challenge earned him a kiss, how much more would she do to him if she did something truly dangerous?

"Um. I guess that was my way of saying thank you." She pulled her hands from his cheeks and gave him a shaky smile.

"Any time you want to thank me like that, Hals, don't hesitate." He leaned in for another taste, but she'd already unbuckled her seat belt and was scrambling from the car.

Damn. He knew it was best to let her go at her own pace, but her pace was notably slower than his own. He was willing, though, especially if she continued to push her own boundaries. He shoved his hand into his hair and followed her, reasoning he could use some fresh air, too.

"Who owns this land?" she asked, shielding her eyes from the bright autumn sunshine.

"Mags Dumond, who else?"

"I wonder why she hasn't done anything with it. It seems like a good area to build a rambling ranch house with stables behind it."

"Maybe the land belonged to an ex-lover or a woman

she didn't get along with in high school. It'd be like Mags not to rebuild out of spite."

The breeze kicked Hallie's hair around her head and Gav crammed his hands in his pockets. He wanted to touch her, but he had a feeling if he did, he'd grab her up and kiss her, this time not coming up for air for several minutes. And if he did that, he wasn't entirely sure she wouldn't drive off and leave him here.

She faced him, her expression contemplative. "Do you think Mags is all bad?"

"Well, she did frame Cash for a DUI because he refused to sign with Cheating Hearts." He supposed it was possible Mags hid a good heart beneath her scaly hide. Unlikely, but possible. "She seems to delight in the downfall of others."

"Those are usually the saddest people." Hallie pinned him with a soft golden gaze and again, he could think of nothing but kissing her, wrapping his palms around her hips and pulling her flush to his body. Then he'd slide his tongue past her lips and drink his fill.

"Hals—"

"We should take the car back." She took a deliberate step away from him, and left him standing there while she shut herself into the passenger side.

He shook his head, the wind ruffling his hair.

"You win this round, Hallie Banks," he mumbled to himself as he opened the driver's-side door.

Next time, all bets were off.

Eight

Hallie parked her sensible used car in the driveway of Cash's mansion. Presley's freshly washed Jeep was on proud display and sparkling in the sunshine, a bucket of soapy water and a hose sitting in a puddle next to it.

Presley had invited Hallie and Cassandra over for pizza and a movie since Cash was going out with Luke and Gavin tonight. Judging by the lack of cars in the driveway, Hallie must've arrived first. No sooner had the thought occurred than a black truck pulled in behind her. Luke had one hand on the wheel and the other on Cassandra's neck. He leaned in and kissed her, and Hallie spun around to give them privacy, turning only when she heard a truck door open and close.

The other woman was cradling two bottles of wine, a stylish bag slung over one shoulder. She was beautiful on any day but looked particularly attractive today with her dark hair pinned back and wearing a ruffly coral-colored dress. Hallie glanced down at her own jeans and black top and instantly felt underdressed.

Until Cassandra said, "I love a scoop neck on you." She pulled Hallie into a quick hug and handed her one of the wine bottles.

"I love your dress," Hallie returned.

"Thanks! It was just something I threw on." On top of being beautiful, put together and humble, Cassandra was an amazingly talented event planner. She'd pulled off Hannah and Will's wedding without a hitch. Or maybe *with a hitch* was the right phrase. Hannah was now officially a Sutherland, though she retained the Banks name for celebrity reasons.

Cassandra blew an air-kiss to her fiancé. Luke waved, a smile on his scruffy face as he pulled out of the driveway, presumably to go meet his brothers.

Hallie raised her hand to knock, but Cassandra twisted the doorknob. "No need to be formal, she is expecting us."

In the foyer of Cash's, and now Presley's, immaculate home, Hallie released a deep breath. It had been a long, strange week. She was ready to relax.

"We are here and we are ready to party!" Cassandra belted out.

Presley was standing in front of the kitchen island—dressed in jeans, thank goodness. She rushed to take the wine bottles. "Perfect! I didn't mean to take the wine before I hug you, but I need a glass after the week I've had."

"Ditto," Hallie agreed.

After wine was poured and hugs were given, they moved to the living room and lounged on the leather couches flanking a tall, stone fireplace. In late autumn, temperatures often dipped into the fifties or cooler, so there was a good chance they would build a fire tonight.

Midway through her first glass of wine, Presley launched into a story about work. As a journalist for Viral Pop, she knew all the entertainment gossip. Just this past summer, her article about Cash had not only landed her a decent raise, but also allowed her to work anywhere in the world. Handy, given she would accompany Cash wherever he toured.

"So anyway," Pres continued, pouring another splash of wine into her glass. "They loved my idea but only *after* I reminded them that my last article was mentioned by at least three different late-show hosts." Everyone raised their glasses in congratulations. She waved a hand. "Enough about me. How have your weeks gone?"

"I have a wedding coming up next month, and even though the bride is picky beyond belief, I've enjoyed planning it. I like a challenge."

"Honey, Luke is proof you *love* a challenge." Presley tapped her wineglass with Cassandra's and they both laughed.

"What about you, Hallie? Anything new?" Cassandra asked.

Hallie opened her mouth to answer, but Presley beat her to it.

"Oh, nothing is new with Hallie at all. Except she asked Gavin to help her loosen up and have some fun.

Her first rule-breaking excursion happened after I pretended I couldn't drive her home and sent her off with him instead." She batted her eyelashes at Hallie. "Sorry, not sorry. And, by the way, you never told me what happened."

Cassandra turned her full attention to Hallie, as well. "I, too, am interested in finding out what happened."

"We went to a dealership to trade in his truck, and then we test-drove a car. That was it." Hallie drank some wine, praying no one would pry. A pipe dream in this group.

"That is not *all*." Pres narrowed her eyes. Which meant she knew something. But what? It was hard to say. She lived with Cash, and Cash and Gavin hung out often. Hallie supposed Gavin could have mentioned their off-roading excursion. But would he have mentioned the spontaneous kiss she'd planted on him?

"He asked me to drive this really expensive sports car," Hallie admitted.

Presley and Cassandra grinned at each other and then spoke in tandem. *"And?"*

"And... He said my first rule to break was to drive over the speed limit. It wasn't a big deal," she said with a nervous laugh. She wasn't used to being the center of attention, even in a crowd of two. She'd admit it was slightly thrilling to have her friends hanging on her every word. "I drove maybe seven or eight miles an hour over."

"Oh. That's...good." Cassandra's smile was almost disappointed.

Well, far be it from Hallie to let down her girls. They wanted something juicier? She had just the thing.

"I stopped the car at the end of a dirt road and then…" she started, pleased when Cassandra and Presley both leaned forward in their seats. "I grabbed his face and… sort of kissed him?"

"You kissed him!" Presley exclaimed. "Way to bury the lede!"

"What kind of a kiss was it?" Cassandra curled her wineglass against her chest.

"Oh, you know." Hallie hesitated, searching her head for the right words. "A basic kiss."

"What is a *basic* kiss?" Presley asked after exchanging glances with Cassandra.

"Well, it was like…" She demonstrated by laying a smacking kiss on the back of her hand and making a "mwah" sound.

"I'm excited there was a kiss at all." Presley insisted. "How did he react?"

"I don't know. I burst out of the car and ran away. I mean, I didn't run away *exactly*, I just got out to look at that old abandoned house at the end of Magnolia Lane."

"That place creeps me out. Cash and I drove back there once to…" Presley blushed prettily and then twirled a lock of her red hair around one finger. "Well. It doesn't matter why we were back there."

"Speak for yourself." Cassandra waggled her eyebrows and Presley giggled.

Hallie, who had only recently broken her first rule, and not a very interesting one, realized her adventure paled in comparison with the ones her friends had experienced. She was beginning to believe she hadn't done anything remotely interesting in her life, which was beyond disappointing.

Did Gavin find her as uninteresting as she felt?

"Let's choose a movie," Cassandra suggested.

"Rom-com?" Presley reached for the remote. "I would love to see the new one about the marriage of convenience between the big, fancy hotel chain owner in Chicago and a woman who owns a boutique hotel down the road."

"Me, too. That actor is *hot*," Cassandra agreed.

Hallie smiled wanly, feeling left out, and not only because she didn't know what movie they were talking about. She was the only single woman in this room, and the highlight of her week—hell, the highlight of her *whole year*—had been the moment she placed a tepid kiss on the center of Gavin's perfect mouth.

Except she couldn't exactly chastise herself for it. The second her lips touched his, she could have melted into him and not come up for air for a good long while. The stubble around his firm lips had tickled hers, and the look in his eyes when she backed away was worth its weight in gold. He'd been surprised, and if she hadn't been mistaken, he'd enjoyed it. Maybe not as much as she had, but close.

As Presley thumbed through the digital menu on the large flat-screen TV hanging over the fireplace, Cassandra microwaved some popcorn. Once the movie started, Hallie curled her leg beneath her and smiled to herself.

She might've downplayed the kiss to her friends, but it'd been much hotter than she'd let on.

Maybe she'd dare herself to do it again the next time she saw him…

At The Cheshire bar atop the Beaumont Hotel, Cash palmed his glass of bourbon and shook his head. "She kissed you to say thanks?"

Gavin lifted his own glass and tilted his head. "Well, that's what she *said*, but I don't think that's why she kissed me."

"Why else would Hallie Banks kiss you?" Luke chimed in.

Cash laughed.

Insulted, Gavin took a sip of his own drink. "Thanks a lot."

They were in one of the private VIP rooms that offered a spectacular view of downtown Beaumont Bay. Luke often reserved one of the suites whenever they hung out together.

"She's not the most outgoing woman we know," Cash said. "You have to admit her kissing you is damn shocking."

Gavin could admit it was shocking, but what he wouldn't admit to his boneheaded brothers was that it was *amazing*. It was a peck of a kiss that shouldn't have ignited him, and yet…

"So what's next?" Luke asked.

"Whatever she wants. I am merely a humble teacher." He splayed his hands on his chest and tried to look innocent. It worked in court sometimes, but never on his brothers. They knew him too well.

"You're not a humble anything," Cash said. "She's not going to be as easy to woo as the women you're used to dating."

"What's that supposed to mean?" Gavin snapped, before realizing he really wanted to know.

"I'm not insulting the women you date, more your method," Cash answered. "The second they present a challenge, you pull away."

"That's not true." But Gavin frowned. Because it felt true.

"You do what comes easy. It's not an insult. It's an observation." Cash shrugged.

"Don't we all do what's easy?" Gavin asked, hoping the question was rhetorical. It wasn't.

"Have you met our fiancées?" Luke deadpanned.

Fair point. Luke had asked Cassandra to bail him out of being named most eligible bachelor by pretending to be his fiancée. Forget that they'd dated years prior and things had not ended well. Cassandra agreed, but only because she wanted a hand in Will and Hannah's wedding. Despite their bumpy start—and bumpier restart— it'd worked out in the end. And then there was Cash, who had been set up—by Gavin, no less—to let Presley stay at his place while writing her article for Viral Pop. Gavin liked to think those two found each other again thanks to him, although Cash hadn't had the decency to thank him for it yet. The jerk.

"I'm not looking to be saddled," Gavin said, his reaction more knee-jerk than authentic.

"Don't knock it till you try it." Luke smirked.

"You know what I mean," Gavin replied before Luke could make a "riding crop" reference.

The idea of someone romantically involved in Gavin's life was fine. The idea of that same someone *permanently* involved was not fine. He had a busy career that consumed a lot of his time. He made room for fun, sure, but planning a family and a future? No, thanks. Not only did that flirt too much with settling down, but it also set him up for a huge fail. A temporary relationship ending with both parties walking away was far easier than untangling the strings of a marriage— or, *gulp*, children. He hated to admit it, even to himself, but he was beginning to believe his brothers were far braver than him in that regard.

"I'm not blind. I know you each have incredible women at your sides, but you have to know you're exceptions to the rule." He slanted a glance at Cash. "You're welcome for Presley, by the way. But not everyone is looking for forever."

"Like we were?" Cash chuffed.

"Dude, you wrote her two songs," Luke chimed in. Gavin was pleased to see Cash's expression of chagrin.

"Hallie is the one who kissed me, so don't accuse me of being predatory. I didn't even kiss her back." Which was less a comment of how chaste he was and more a comment of how she'd surprised the hell out of him, but still.

"And if she kisses you again?" Luke raised his eyebrows.

Gavin shrugged. "If she's interested in more, why not?"

"Uh, a million reasons?" Cash said. "The main one being your brother is married to her twin sister."

"Hallie's her own person." Gavin was beginning to understand how irritating it must be for her to be lumped in with Hannah all the time. Though he'd lumped her in with her twin as a reason not to give in to his attraction to her, hadn't he? Well. That was ridiculous. Hallie was an adult. *He* was an adult. If they wanted to do naked, sweaty, scintillating adult things to each other and never look back, that was their prerogative.

"Yeah, and Will's got a mean right hook," Luke put in. He poured himself a bourbon and sat on a bar stool, a backdrop of liquor bottles behind him.

"She was the one who asked me to help her step out of her comfort zone. I'm going to give her what she asked for." Gavin sipped his drink. "Whatever that entails."

"Your funeral," Cash said, and then Luke drank to that.

Nine

Hallie didn't make a habit of drinking too much, but she'd had such a good time with Presley and Cassandra last night she'd accidentally overindulged. She arrived at Gavin's new house with a headache and a very large cup of coffee. She supposed she could've put him off for another day or two, but that wasn't her style. She'd promised to be here at nine thirty in the morning, so here she was, at 9:27 a.m. He needed her help, after all.

And a few more kisses, her mind happily suggested.

The more she thought about kissing him, the more nervous she became. She couldn't very well attack him when he answered the door, now could she? And she was terrified to ask for a kiss. What if he responded with an apologetic refusal? She'd *die*. Which meant if they did kiss, it'd have to be unplanned—like the first time she'd kissed him. The spontaneous kiss had worked out okay. She thought.

The driveway curved through two lines of tall trees, sun filtering through their leaves. When those trees gave way to the house, she gasped.

Gavin's droolworthy home was perched on a slight incline overlooking both the main lake as well as the smaller, private lake that he owned a portion of. The log cabin–style A-frame was enormous, with copious windows and several balconies.

She stepped from her car and craned her head to take in a wide balcony on the second floor. Beyond a pair of double doors rose high cathedral ceilings. "Wow," she heard herself whisper. Someone else heard her, as well.

"She's beautiful, isn't she?"

Startled by Gavin's sudden appearance next to her, she jolted, placing her hand over her racing heart as she gave him a smile. "Where did you come from? You scared the life out of me."

"You look plenty alive to me, Hals." He grinned, his gaze briefly flicking to her lips before returning to the house. His place wasn't quite as big as Cash's sprawling mansion but was in no way quaint. "Fifty-three hundred square feet," he said as if reading her mind.

"How many people are going to live here with you?" she teased.

"I know, right? The plans made it seem smaller. Come on, I'll show you around."

She followed him in, walking up a short set of stairs to the front door. That door opened to an enormous kitchen and living room. The bold, dark wooden beams overhead were modern, charcoal gray set against a backdrop of pale pine.

"I paid extra for those." On anyone else it would've sounded like a brag, but she knew Gavin was simply being conversational. She'd always admired his ability to simply say what he thought. She overthought everything.

"Well, they were worth it." She stepped into the kitchen and stood between two massive islands, each with their own built-in sinks. Black bar stools were pushed beneath the overhang of one of the islands, each seat tall and padded, with shining silver rivets bolted into the leather.

"Clearly nothing needs to be done in this room," she said as she took in the gorgeous space. Behind the glass-doored cabinets were rows of cookbooks and canisters, as if every detail had already been decided.

"The kitchen is the only part of the house that *is* done. Come with me."

After a tour of the bedrooms—she was still trying to wrap her head around why he had six of them—she saw what Gavin meant. Two bedrooms were unfurnished, and the others weren't furnished to capacity.

In the master bedroom's walk-in closet, she smiled at the array of mismatched plastic hangers. She pointed at him with a turquoise blue one. "Tell me this is on your designer's list."

"You're in charge of this mess, not me." He took the hanger, bringing him a step closer to her. The closet wasn't small but seemed to shrink when he leaned one shoulder on the door frame and gave her a sexy grin.

"Wooden hangers," she managed, clearing her throat and her head of the idea of kissing him again. Standing over her, he was almost imposing. When he'd been across from her in the car, she'd been eye to eye with him. There had been no need to push to her toes or drag his mouth down to hers. Both of which she'd have to do if she kissed him now. Was it hot in here? She tore her eyes from his tempting frame to admire the built-in shelves and silver rods where his clothes hung in no particular order. "Dark brown or black hangers would be best."

She removed a suit jacket from in between two shirts and hung it with the other jackets, and then she moved a pair of suit pants to the lower rung before she realized what she was doing was strangely intimate.

"Sorry." She backed away from his clothes. "I didn't mean to invade your space."

"Don't be." He straightened from the door frame and stepped deeper into the closet, his lips flinching as he looked at her lips again. "You invaded my space once before. You didn't hear me complaining, did you?"

Heat flushed her neck and face when he leaned a hair's breadth closer. Maybe she wouldn't have to initiate their next kiss. He was going to do it for her. She tipped her chin to accept what he was about to offer when a female voice punctuated the air.

"Yoo-hoo! Gav?"

Head still tilted downward, he didn't move an inch, but Hallie did. She sprang away from him and darted out of the closet as a tall, dark-skinned woman stepped into the bedroom.

"You must be Ruby," Hallie said as Gavin came to stand next to her.

"Yes. I am." Ruby propped a hand on one of her hips, her expression curious as it snapped from Hallie to Gavin. The other woman was showing off her curves in an exotically patterned dress, her shoes tall and strappy.

"This is Hallie," Gavin introduced. "She's going to be handling any and all questions you may have about decorating this beast."

"Really." Ruby's pink lips pulled into an almost smile, her shrewd but friendly eyes taking in Hallie slowly. She tilted her head at Gavin. "I didn't realize you were seeing someone."

Ruby, with her bright green purse and glittery nail polish, seemed a better dating option for outgoing Gavin than Hallie.

"She knows what she's doing." His arm hugged Hallie's shoulders. She stiffened against him, surprised when he didn't correct Ruby's assumption. "I trust her."

"Well. Then let's get started," Ruby said.

They tracked down the hallway, Gavin keeping his palm loosely pressed to Hallie's lower back while Ruby chatted about her ideas for each room. Hallie was beginning to understand why he had needed help. She was already overwhelmed and she'd been in Ruby's presence for a mere ten minutes.

Downstairs, Gavin backed out of the kitchen, his palms clasped together. "I'm going to take off if you two have it under control. Hals, you'll call me if you need anything?"

"Of course. Yes."

"Great. Ruby. Always a pleasure." With that he was off, the door shutting behind him. Hallie watched out one of the giant windows as he pulled away in the same F-150 he'd had the day they'd test driven the red car. He'd told Chad he hadn't been quite ready to trade the truck in yet. The salesman was understandably disappointed, but covered with a toothy smile, promising Gavin he'd find him the perfect ride.

"How new is it?" Ruby asked.

"The truck? I think a little over a year. He was going to trade it in, but he ended up keeping it. He likes the color gray."

Ruby laughed, the sound throaty. "I meant you and Gavin seeing each other. How new is it?"

Oh. That. They weren't seeing each other, but since he hadn't corrected Ruby, Hallie felt as if she'd be breaking some sort of unspoken confidence if she denied it. "We haven't been hanging out long, but we've known each other for a while."

There. That was safe.

"What about you? How long have you known Gavin?"

Ruby regarded the beamed ceiling before jotting something into a small notebook. "Eleven, twelve years? Somewhere in there."

Hallie felt her mouth form a perfect O.

"We studied prelaw together. I was going to be a lawyer when I grew up, but I changed my major."

"To interior design."

"Yep. Much more fun." Ruby winked. "So, your sister married Gavin's brother and you're dating Gavin.

You two always keep your romantic interests in the family?"

Ruby's curiosity was natural, but resentment burbled to the surface anyway. Hallie was tired of being lumped in with her twin. As if she simply followed Hannah's lead and didn't make any decisions for herself. Rather than be rude, Hallie covered with, "They can tell us apart, so no issues there."

"Sorry, I didn't mean to insult you." The other woman's smile was gentle and Hallie waved her off, realizing she'd taken Ruby's remark personally. "We didn't date or anything—Gavin and me—in case you were wondering."

Hallie had been wondering but hadn't wanted to pry. Plus, she liked to think if she and Gavin were *actually* dating, he'd have told her about dating Ruby prior to introducing them.

Ruby set her handbag down and rummaged through it. "He raced out of here before I could show him these. Was this what scared him off?" She tossed a giant stack of fabric swatches, held together with a metal ring, onto the countertop.

Hallie thumbed the stitching on one of the swatches. "Curtains?"

"Unless he'd rather have bamboo blinds. Or those fancy screens outfitted with a remote, but I would never suggest hiding this view."

Hallie and Ruby struck an easy camaraderie from there. By afternoon they were excitedly sharing ideas and deciding on fabric. Craving a cup of coffee herself,

Hallie offered Ruby one, as well. They settled at the massive countertop, mugs in hand.

"He had his priorities straight when he chose that fancy-ass espresso machine," Ruby quipped.

"Agreed." Not only did the machine grind the beans, but it also brewed the coffee and then frothed the milk automatically.

"I have to admit, I wasn't sure what to think when Gavin handed me off to you." Ruby cocked her head, her expression quizzical. "You know his style well for not having been seeing him long."

Hallie laughed, slightly uncomfortable that Ruby had noticed. "He's been in my periphery for a while."

"I can see why." Ruby sipped her coffee. "He's yummy. Decorating someone's home is an intimate act. He must trust you."

"It's just a favor."

"I bet it is." Ruby elbowed Hallie, her laugh slightly lecherous. "You make sure he does you a few *favors* in the bedroom tonight as a reward for how well you did with me today."

Hallie grimaced and, of course, observant Ruby noticed. The other woman's eyebrows leaped up her forehead. "Don't tell me it's so new that you haven't…"

"Um…" Hallie studied her own coffee.

"Me and my big mouth. Ignore me, please. I didn't mean to make you uncomfortable."

"I'm not," Hallie said—at least not for the reason Ruby thought. "We're taking things slow."

"Slow is good for relationships. For design, not so much. You ready to check out the downstairs patio? I have a few ideas for furniture and your man will not commit to a style."

The idea of Gavin as *her man* was as titillating as the idea of them going to bed together tonight, but the reminder of him not committing was sobering. No matter what lines and boundaries Hallie crossed with the sexy lawyer, she'd do well to remember all good things came to an end. When their rule-breaking tête-à-tête reached its apex, so too would whatever was simmering between them.

Ten

To thank Hallie for her help this week, Gavin made reservations for them at the Silver Marmot, an upscale steak house downtown, a regular hangout for him.

The atmosphere was perfect for private conversations as well as romantic ones. If one was inclined to romance. He was beginning to think Hallie *wasn't*, given the direction she'd steered the conversation.

"It's the coolest toilet I've ever seen."

He coughed into his glass and nearly spit red wine on his shirt. She'd been going on about the master bedroom's shower, supersize with a bench and multiple sprayers. Just when he'd lapsed into a fantasy involving her beneath those sprayers, her naked body pressed to his, she mentioned the toilet.

"Sorry." She sent a quick look around the restaurant. "I was carried away."

He'd say. Ever since they sat down, she'd adorably reassured him that she didn't steer Ruby wrong with the choices she'd made for his house.

"Don't be sorry." Her interrupting his shower fantasy aside, he meant it. "I was sincere when I said I trusted you. I'm sure you did a great job."

She smiled prettily as she sliced into her filet mignon. The restaurant's limited autumn menu featured additional toppings for the fine cut of beef. Gavin had chosen shrimp and clarified butter for his steak, while Hallie went with blue cheese and fried sage.

"I didn't mean to talk about the toilet at dinner." She ate a bite of steak. He watched her plump lips close over the fork, weirdly turned on by the idea that she hadn't balked at the idea of steak. He had no problems with women who ate salads for dinner, but he preferred a woman who satisfied her appetite. In *every* way.

"Ruby said you nailed my style." He popped a shrimp into his mouth, intrigued by the fact that Hallie knew what he liked. "How so?"

"Um." She concentrated way too hard on stabbing a piece of broccoli. "I just…pay attention to details."

"About me?" he fished.

"Sure." She shrugged.

He couldn't help grinning. "Like what?"

"Like the way you dress." She gestured at him with her fork. "You favor the same style of shirt and pair it with an immaculately tailored jacket and trousers."

He liked hearing she'd noticed him below the waist, but it was probably best not to say that out loud.

"Your desk is tidy, with only a few streamlined necessities on it. Odd, really," she said almost to herself before taking another bite of her dinner.

"What's odd about it?" He was curious now.

She finished chewing before taking a swallow of red wine. "Well, you're not neat at home. I'm not saying you're a slob, but in your closet, the clothes are hanging everywhere in no discernible order. Which was why I was rearranging them. Jackets. Shirts. Trousers. Ties." She sliced the air with her hand as she said each word.

"I am not surprised you like order, Hals," he said with a soft laugh. "What's your closet look like?"

"It's overflowing with clothes. Mostly neutrals and professional styles."

"And the dress you looked so hot in a few weeks back," he added.

She sent him a smile he felt in his gut. "Yes, among others I don't wear."

He found that very interesting. So interesting, he leaned forward in his chair. "Explain."

She took a deep breath. "Hannah gives me her castoffs. Some dresses she's worn for photos and doesn't want to be photographed in them again. Others she never wore but thought suited me. Honestly, though, where would I wear fancy dresses?"

"Out to dinner." He regarded her black suit jacket and blouse. "Not that I don't like what you're wearing tonight. I do. Your hair looks bright against black and your eyes appear more golden. Your skin is glowing."

Her mouth dropped open gently. He loved surprising her, if only for that reaction right there.

"If you like the dresses enough to keep them in your closet, you should wear them. To work. To lunch. While doing housework."

The joke caught her off guard and she laughed full out, drawing a few gazes from diners at another table. Damn, he liked the carefree sound way too much.

"Could you imagine me in a sequined royal blue gown while running the vacuum?"

She'd moved to reclaim her knife, but he reached over and took her hand before she could. When he had her full attention, he said, "I can imagine you lots of ways. It's about time you started doing the same."

Her fingers flinched in his and the air around them charged with sharp sexual energy. He felt it as sure as the chair under his ass. She must have, too. The levity from earlier was gone, replaced by something far more potent. And *really* welcome.

He released her hand and moved on to more innocuous topics while they finished their dinners. When the waiter brought by the dessert tray, Hallie politely refused. Gavin did not.

"Have a bite," he said when a tall slice of layered chocolate cake was set between them.

"I can't."

"Why not?" There seemed to be a lot of things Hallie "couldn't" do. Like kiss him in his closet when Ruby was in the other room, or eat dessert, or wear dresses she wanted to wear. He didn't like the way she limited herself. He wanted her to let loose, especially with him.

"I'm stuffed."

"You barely ate half your steak. You still have wine in your glass. I insist." He spooned up a bite of cake and held it toward her mouth. She quirked her lips in a show of doubt. He waggled the spoon. "I can do this all day."

She rolled her eyes but gave in, leaning forward and opening her mouth. He fed her the cake, and she closed her eyes and hummed low in her throat. He froze watching the display, the spoon hovering in midair. When she darted her tongue out to lick her lips, he felt it in places much lower than his gut.

Because, *damn*.

"You know." She dabbed her mouth with the napkin, her tone far too light for the intensity weighing down his chest. "I'm surprised you didn't bring home the red sports car. Are you more attached to your truck than you care to admit?"

"I don't become attached. It's my superpower." His glib answer earned a subtle nod from Hallie, but not one of agreement.

"You drove that red race car like you loved it. And yet we left in the same charcoal-gray truck we arrived in."

Yeah, well, he'd been too distracted by the kiss she'd laid on his mouth to trust himself with a decision as big as buying a car. He didn't have an issue with paying sticker for a brand-new vehicle, even one as expensive as that one, but he refused to sign on the dotted line when he wasn't in possession of his faculties.

"I'm not saying this because I think you should buy it," she added, though he suddenly felt properly challenged to do just that first thing tomorrow morning. "I'm saying it because you really enjoyed driving that car. Likewise, your home should reflect all sides of you. The neat, meticulous, though moderately unorganized side." She winked at him and he found he liked this confident side of her most. "And the side that lets loose to enjoy something just because."

Meaning enjoying something without weighing the future, or what might happen if he gave in? Because that's the direction his mind had gone.

"So you approve of letting loose in my house?" he asked, his voice a low rumble.

"Decoratively speaking." She blushed, but he guessed she knew exactly what he'd been getting at. "Don't be alarmed when you tour your rooms and find a rare, vibrant punch of color every so often. I might've chosen focal points simply because they're unexpected. Each room should feel as exciting as when you were handed the keys to that shiny red sports car."

Her shoulders had pulled back while she was speaking, her eyes glinting in the candlelight. She was proud of herself and hell, she should be. She had described him almost better than he could have described himself.

"You're incredible," he murmured.

"Just observant." Her eyes dashed away.

"Incredibly observant," he amended, reaching for her hand again. She accepted the compliment without argument this time.

He ate a bite of the decadent cake. "Damn. That is good." He licked the spoon, noticing when Hallie noticed him do it. He was so glad he'd asked her out—glad he'd spent time with her outside of work. She was not only smart and professional, but interesting *and* beautiful. A quadruple threat.

Normally, he preferred a clearly marked boundary

line between his private life and the women in it. He wasn't a *manwhore* or anything, but he tended to keep the company of the same woman to a minimum. And that never included a woman accompanying him car shopping or choosing his window treatments.

Familiarity might explain his comfort level with Hallie, but it sure didn't explain the punch of attraction that nearly TKO'd him. She was easy to talk to, fun to hang out with, and she intrigued the hell out of him. Why *did* she have a closet full of clothes she refused to wear? Why *had* she avoided him like the bubonic plague until now? And why was she suddenly interested in breaking rules when she was clearly more comfortable walking the line?

He couldn't remember being interested in more than the present moment with the women he'd previously dated. They'd discussed dinner plans and current events. Sometimes work. But he couldn't recall staring at the ceiling for hours replaying a kiss that never led to more.

He ate another big bite of cake. He'd thought he lived his life to the fullest in every area, but her suggesting his home didn't reflect that made him wonder if he'd held back in some areas. Hallie had asked him to be her teacher. He owed it to her to be a good example of letting loose. Including and especially with her.

He offered her the remainder of the cake, which she refused, so he ate it. "Hals. You're going to have to break a few more rules if you want to make progress."

When she asked what he meant, he scraped the last of the frosting off the plate and said, "You'll see."

Eleven

Hallie didn't know what Gavin's "you'll see" comment referred to, but after dinner they didn't go straight to his truck so he could drive her home. Instead, he angled away from the sidewalk leading through town and toward the water behind the row of restaurants and shops.

The night was moonlit, the stars shimmering. Laughter echoed off the water, interspersed by the low blubber of boat motorists who honored the "no wake" restriction after sundown.

On a boardwalk along the lake's shoreline, vendors in booths and food trucks sold fall-themed treats. From pumpkin bread to caramel apples to funnel cake, there was a lot to choose from.

"Does your sweet tooth beckon?" Hallie teased as they passed by another vendor.

"Yes. Especially the apple covered in chocolate drizzle and marshmallows. Too bad I ate dessert already."

"I didn't peg you for a marshmallow guy."

"I'm sweeter than you think." His grin was flirty. "What about you? What's the real reason behind you thwarting my efforts to split dessert with you? And you'd better not say you're dieting."

"I told you the real reason. Dinner was filling." Plus, she didn't want to stuff herself and feel sluggish. She might miss something—like this lovely walk. Or whatever happened later... "The bite you gave me was perfect. Sometimes a taste is just enough."

"And sometimes, a taste only makes you want more." He turned and she stopped short, tipping her head to look up at him. His hair blew softly in the breeze rolling off the water, tempting her to tousle what she imagined would be soft, wavy strands.

He reached down and grasped her hand, tugging her closer to him to avoid an oncoming couple. "This okay?" he asked, their arms touching from elbows to palms.

"Yeah. Yes." Far better than okay.

The locals thwarted the autumn chill in the air with light jackets. Others, likely tourists from warmer climates, wore thicker coats and scarves.

Gavin paused in front of a display window of a luxury shop. "I buy my suits here. I'd be lost without my tailor. He helps me step into the role of cutthroat lawyer."

"You should call him your *costumer*." She laughed. "A cutthroat anything is so not you."

"As a fun-loving, likable guy, I have to overcompensate. Better for my clients that I'm mistaken for a lion than a lamb."

"I like that about you," she blurted out before she'd meant to. She shut her eyes and smiled to herself. "When it came to choosing between fun or hardworking, guess what I chose?"

"It doesn't mean you can't choose again." He tucked her hair behind her ear, lingering to trace her cheek with one finger. She wanted to lean into his hand, push to her toes and taste his mouth. She didn't, though, which only proved how far she had to go. "You don't have to fit a mold, Hals. Not one assigned to you by society or formed by expectations. From others or from your sister."

"Normally I'd be worried about this." She lifted their joined hands.

"Holding my hand?"

"I'm mistaken for Hannah in public often. Now she's married. And here I am with her husband's brother. If the tabloids spotted us, they'd go crazy."

"Any of them here now?" He glanced around.

"I'm not sure," she said, inspecting the people milling around. "Usually you can tell by the way they peek and quickly look away. Or when they whisper to whomever they're with before discreetly snapping a photo."

"Sounds like a pain in the ass." He pulled her around to stand in front of him.

"I'm used to it."

"Used to holding back for the sake of your sister's reputation?"

She hated to admit how right he was, but that was exactly what she'd been doing.

"Used to them assuming I'm Hannah."

"Oh, but they're wrong. Instead they're getting a rare peek at her more elusive, insanely gorgeous, fun, intelligent, brave sister, Hallie Banks. They won't know what to do with themselves." His mouth tipped up on one side, making him look boyish and manly at the same time. "I'm having that issue myself."

Again with the compliments. She didn't know what to do with herself when he talked to her like that. Tearing off his clothes seemed a tad dramatic, but the temptation was there all the same.

He smiled down at her, revealing a fan of smile lines at the corners of his eyes. Then he grasped both her hands in his. "Is this okay, too?" His voice dropped an octave, not only quieter but also huskier.

"It's a little backward. Hand-holding typically precludes a kiss. I already kissed you."

"I recall. It's all I've been able to think about since it happened."

Same. She melted toward him another inch. "Really?"

"Really. I wasn't ready last time. I demand a do-over."

"I guess I did sort of…attack you. That wasn't like me. I was excited."

"I like making you excited. And, for the record, I think that was like you. It's the *you* that you refuse to let come out and play. Ready to break another rule, Hallie?"

"The hand-holding doesn't count?" she whispered, knowing it didn't.

"Sorry, sweetheart. You're going to have to do better than that." His smile emboldened her. "This time, I encourage you to go *all in* on the attack part."

Her heart hit her throat and she honestly couldn't tell if she was excited or nervous. Maybe both. "This is a *very* public venue, Gav."

"So?" He checked their surroundings again while she did the same. No one appeared to be looking their direction, furtively or otherwise.

"They're watching. I can feel them."

"Well, then," he murmured. "We should give them something to see."

His gaze zoomed unerringly on her mouth. Then those gray-blue eyes trickled back up to hers and his smile snapped into place like it'd never left. How could she resist his invitation?

Simple. She couldn't.

She draped her arms onto his wide shoulders, stepping so close they were touching from chest to hips.

"Is this okay?" she repeated his earlier question, hardly recognizing the boldness of her own voice.

His next exhalation fanned her hair from her forehead as his hands squeezed her hips. "*So* okay."

Then she pushed to her toes and set her mouth to his.

Gavin had asked for an attack hoping she'd throw herself at him in a blur of tongue, teeth and lips. What he received was ten times better.

Hallie was flush against him, her hands climbing his

neck and her fingers toying with the ends of his hair. Her lips moved on his, slow but sure, her plush mouth firm yet yielding. She didn't simply press a kiss into his mouth and move away, no, no. She *lingered*.

Worries of being watched or photographed were a distant memory. He didn't give a shit if they'd inadvertently started an international scandal.

Hallie deserved moments like this one. Moments where she prioritized what she wanted. Moments where she whimpered into his mouth as her tongue tangled with his. Her breasts smashed against his chest and even with her jacket between them, he could make out her curves. This kiss was different from the spontaneous one in the car on that back road. She was taking what she wanted for no other reason than she wanted it. He was proud of her.

To show his appreciation, he tipped his head and opened his mouth wider, inviting her to continue. To his shock, she did. Right in front of a storefront window in the middle of the shopping district in Beaumont Bay, she kissed him like she was famished and he was the only sustenance that would suffice.

He ended up pulling his mouth from hers, only because his erection was going to become obvious to passersby if he didn't wrangle in his libido.

Panting, he tightened his grasp around her arms and gave her a severe look. One he hoped communicated his need to get the hell out of here and go somewhere private where they could continue what she'd started.

If this was how hot he felt while kissing her, he could

only imagine what would happen if they were naked together. The top of his head might blow clean off.

Through glazed eyes and a wonky smile, Hallie resembled a woman who would say yes to whatever he asked. So, he asked.

"Why don't we—"

"Oh my God, is that Hannah Banks?" someone said.

"And Will Sutherland's brother!" someone else chimed in.

Hallie's hazy, happy expression snapped back to the veiled one she normally wore. He was losing her, which was unacceptable. He had bigger, better plans for her tonight. He refused to let the feistier version of her go.

"She's—" he started only to be interrupted by Hallie.

"Hallie Banks. Hannah's twin," she finished for him. "Hannah is traveling."

"Sorry," one of those someones called out. The crowd practically evaporated, no one caring now that they hadn't caught famous Hannah Banks cheating on her husband.

"Told you," Hallie's smile was nervous. "That's what happens when I don't worry about what happens."

"Hals?"

"Yes?"

He'd been planning to argue in favor of continuing where they'd left off, but in the end, he didn't want to waste his breath on words. So he dived in for another kiss, instead, having no idea how she'd react. Lucky for him, she looped her arms around his neck and kissed him back.

Twelve

Part of her warned herself not to go home with him, but when he offered a nightcap at his place, she couldn't make herself say no. She wanted him, and that wanting had increased tenfold since the day she'd first kissed him.

Gavin helped her down from the tall seat of his truck, keeping hold of her hand as he led her inside and to a corner of the kitchen.

"Coffee or brandy?" He didn't open the cabinet holding various mugs and glassware, but instead twirled a lock of her hair around his fingertip.

Figuring coffee would enhance her jittery nerves, she said, "Brandy."

He poured the liquor into two snifters and handed her one, tapping his glass against hers. She sipped while watching him over the rim, admiring the firm set of his jaw and the warmth lingering in his storm-colored eyes.

"I'm so damn attracted to you," he murmured.

"You took the words out of my mouth."

"I'd better check to make sure." He cupped her waist and lowered his mouth. She tasted brandy on his tongue, mingling with her own desire for him.

"Is this too fast?" he asked between kisses.

"No." She fisted the front of his shirt, dragging him closer.

"Good." He set aside his glass and hers and moved his hands to her jaw. He lit her up with another kiss before backing her across the kitchen where her ass encountered a hard marble countertop.

"Hals…" he started, she assumed to ask if going further was okay. It was more than okay. They'd started something she didn't want to stop, and by the way his eyes were burning into hers, his hands gripping her waist, she could guess he felt the same way.

"Yes." She clung to him, her legs intertwined with his, their bodies glued together over their inconvenient clothing. "Let's not overthink this. Let's do it."

"Sounds good to me," he said, his voice gruff. He cuffed her under the armpits and plopped her butt onto the countertop. She kicked off her shoes and wrestled out of her jacket, so excited—almost *too* excited. His deep chuckle echoed around them and she stilled.

"Am I…doing something wrong?"

"You couldn't possibly do anything wrong." His smile faded as he reached for her coat. "Let me, okay? I've been wanting to unwrap you for a while now."

"Okay," she agreed on a breath.

He moved her jacket off her shoulders and she pulled her arms free. Then he fingered the buttons of her blouse, undoing the top two and kissing her neck. She tilted her head to give him better access. He took liberal advantage, kissing along her collarbone and undoing another button. "Still okay?" he mumbled before sliding his tongue into the space between her breasts.

"Uh-huh," she breathed, clutching the back of his head.

She felt his smile and the warm exhale of his breath against her skin when he said, "Good."

He tugged her shirt open and she wrapped her legs at the backs of his thighs and squeezed. His gray-blue eyes didn't move from hers when he unbuckled the slim belt around her waist. They didn't stray when he unbuttoned and unzipped her, or when she lifted her legs and allowed him to take off her jeans.

When she was down to her bra and panties his gaze wandered over her body. She arched her back and hoped he liked what he saw. Holding her breath, she waited for his reaction. It was a good one.

His nostrils flared, his palm smoothing along her side and up and over one of her breasts. "My God, you're more beautiful than I imagined."

"You imagined?" She reached for the hem of his shirt, tickling his heated skin with her fingertips.

"Honey, you have no idea." He pressed his mouth to hers but she pulled away, tugging at his shirt impatiently.

"I want to see you."

He granted her wish, undoing the buttons on his shirt one by one. As his shirt parted, she was rewarded with muscular pecs and a whirl of dark chest hair. She spread her hands over his heated skin and moaned her approval.

"Like what you see?"

"So much."

"Your turn." He tossed his shirt over his shoulder and reached for her bra, unhooking it and slipping it from her arms. He backed away and admired her breasts before teasing her nipples between his fingers and thumbs. Her skin puckered in the cooler air of the room, as her breaths reduced to harsh exhales of desire.

When he laid his tongue on her skin, she nearly shot off the countertop.

"Relax," he breathed over her damp skin. "I'm in no hurry. I'm not going anywhere. And if you want me to stop—"

She fisted his hair and brought his head up. "Don't you dare."

"Yes, ma'am." He gave her a knee-weakening grin before laving her with his tongue. Long, wet strokes that had her squirming where she sat.

"Now, Gav. Now, now." She'd have been embarrassed to beg before, but she couldn't make herself care now. It'd been far too long since she'd had sex, and she could already tell sex with him was going to be really, *really* great.

"All right, all right," he said, a smile in his voice. He yanked off his pants and then rolled her underwear down, tossing them to the floor with the rest of their clothes.

The backdrop of the shiny, pristine kitchen was beautiful, but not as beautiful as the man between her legs.

His hands wrapped around her ass, he scooted her to the edge of the countertop and dived into her mouth tongue-first. When he kissed her neck, she stole a peek at his penis—erect and long, thick and damn mouthwatering. She couldn't think of anything except what he'd feel like moving inside her. Like every fantasy she'd had come true, she imagined. Mere inches away from that happening, he stopped and blew out what sounded like a tortured breath.

"What's wrong?" she asked, prepared to remind him that he promised not to go anywhere.

"Condom. Hals." He blinked hard. She loved that he'd been as lost in her as she'd been in him. "I need to sheath up, sweetheart."

Fingers in his hair, she tugged gently. "You do?"

His laugh was pure anguish. "Yeah, honey. I do."

"I'm on the pill." She dug her heels into his butt and pulled him against her center. "Do you ever have unprotected sex?"

"Never. It's against my rules." Half his mouth shifted into a smile. "You?"

"I haven't, ah, been in the game for a while, but I have been on birth control pills since I was a teen." For irregular periods that were as far from clockwork as imaginable, but she kept the unsexy detail to herself. "And I never have unprotected sex. Can we count this as a rule to break? Sounds like we can do it safely."

She wasn't sure what the future held for her and

Gavin, but if this was the only chance she had to be with him, she'd gladly forgo a layer of latex between them.

"Skin to skin." He rubbed his bare chest against hers. "Is that what you want?"

"If that's not too selfish." She turned her eyes to his, pleased when his squinted into a smile.

"Not selfish. I want you the same way." He cupped her cheek and delivered a soft kiss to her mouth. "You trust me?"

"Yes."

"Good." The word was practically his motto. He brushed her entrance with the tip of his cock. She gasped, gripping his shoulders and tipping her hips toward his advancing body. He blew out a harsh breath, his eyes dark and molten. "Damn, Hals. That's better than good."

"So much better," she agreed.

He slid deeper, his breath turning ragged. His eyes slipped closed, but she kept hers open, not wanting to miss a single moment. When he dragged out and entered her again, though, her eyes sank shut on their own. He thrust again and again, taking her against the hard countertop. He flattened his hands on her back and brought her body to his, lowering his head to suckle her nipples. Her mind blanked when he nipped her neck, and when he nibbled her earlobe, tremors shook her legs.

"Close?" he breathed, moving frantically with her.

"So close." Her skin caught fire when he lifted her hips and sped up the pace. Within seconds she shouted his name, clutched and came. "You, you," she murmured as her orgasm shimmered through her.

"Right here. Almost," he breathed against her lips.

Her limbs buzzed and her mind blanked as his slick skin slipped along hers. A sheen of sweat decorated his brow as he worked. She shifted her hips, which had the added bonus of him landing deeper. She'd done that for him, but her body greedily took another orgasm. When she let go this time, he went with her. His arms tightened around her before his muscles loosened, and he hissed between his teeth.

The upper half of his body collapsed on hers, his exhalations warm on her throat. She stroked his hair away from his temple. When a full-body shudder overtook him, she committed that to memory, as well.

He kissed her collarbone and her neck before lifting his head. Long lashes shadowed his cheeks, and his full mouth parted to suck in a desperate breath of oxygen. He looked a little lost and a lot impressed when he murmured, *"God damn."*

The profanity was as good as a compliment. She'd reduced this big, strong, confident man into a sated, boneless heap. How much did she love *that*? Of course, she could give him credit for leaving her boneless, as well. She had no idea how she'd find the energy to hop down from this counter and redress herself. Maybe she would slide into a puddle and sleep curled up on the floor instead.

"Hallie, Hallie." He dropped his forehead onto hers. "Incredible. You sounded like you enjoyed yourself. Twice," he added cockily.

"Well, you're very good," she said, happily feeding his ego.

His grin suggested he liked having his ego stroked.

"I have a confession," she whispered as he eased from her body.

His eyebrows lifted.

"I like dessert after sex. Ice cream if you have it."

His grin was slow and satisfied and she thought she'd like to see that exact look on him a few more times. "Cone or bowl?"

"Bowl."

"Whipped cream? Chocolate sauce?" His eyes moved over her naked body. "We should have started with that."

Playing it cool—as if toe-curling sex with him *hadn't* been the highlight of her year—she patted his cheek. "Maybe next time."

Thirteen

"It was irresponsible. And stupid. And it won't happen again." Fingers nested in her blond hair, Hallie hunched over her speakerphone at her desk and prayed her sister wouldn't fire her.

Photos of Hallie and Gavin had popped up on social media shortly after their impromptu make-out sesh on the boardwalk. Telling the crowd she wasn't her sister hadn't prevented at least one person from selling the photos to the highest bidder. The fake story—that Hannah was a cheater and Gavin was the scum of the earth—had probably broken the internet by now.

"I'm *so* sorry, Han." Hallie bristled, but her sister's reaction wasn't the one she'd been expecting. Hannah burst out laughing. "Are you… Are you all right?"

Hannah snorted through another peal of laughter.

Oh-kay. "I assumed you'd be upset learning the world believes you're an adulteress who is cheating on your new husband with his brother."

"Hallie, hon," came Hannah's consoling, comforting voice all the way from France. "Will and I were posting online photos of our vacay at that *exact* moment. Our whereabouts are corroborated and time-stamped. There are several of my fans arguing in my defense—they know those photos are of you and Gavin and not me."

"Oh. Well, that's good news." She'd never considered the PR nightmare could work itself out. "I love your fans."

"Me, too."

Hallie sighed. "For what it's worth, I wasn't trying to start a scandal."

"I can see exactly what you were trying to start." Hannah's tone was salacious. "Are you going to indulge me with details about why you were sliding lips with Gavin Sutherland?"

In the background, Will asked, "Who is that?"

"Don't tell him!" Hallie said at the same time Hannah happily supplied, "Hallie."

"Hannah!"

"The whole world knows you were kissing him. Will would find out eventually. Which begs the question, why were you strolling on the boardwalk with Gavin?"

"He took me to dinner. As a thank-you. I've been helping him with the interior design for his new house."

"And then last night you decided to measure the square footage of his mouth?" Hannah laughed at her own joke. Will groaned.

No way was Hallie telling her sister she'd ended up having condom-less sex with Gavin on his countertop. For one, Hallie wasn't sure she was ready to admit it out loud and for another, she *really* wasn't ready for Will to know about it.

"Don't worry about a thing," Hannah said when Hallie didn't respond. "You know the public. They're going to think what they're going to think. Like Gram always says, we are in charge of how we react."

"You're right." Hallie had conveniently forgotten the wisdom their grandmother had shared repeatedly over the years. In Hallie's defense, whenever Gavin kissed her, she forgot everything.

"I'm always right," Hannah said.

"Square footage of his mouth," Hallie repeated with a smile. Her sister was pretty funny.

"When was the last time you went after what you wanted?" Hannah asked tenderly. "Maybe it's time you allowed yourself to take a risk."

The truth was Hallie had gone after what she'd wanted mere hours ago in Gavin's newly christened kitchen. She ended the call, still smiling both at her sister's reaction and her own warm memories of last night.

Hallie had mentioned a next time and he hadn't argued. Instead, he'd made a giant ice cream sundae smothered in caramel sauce, hot fudge and whipped cream. He'd fed her bites while she sat on the same countertop where they'd had sex.

She'd never look at a bowl of ice cream the same way again.

Before Gavin, she'd convinced herself she wasn't

missing out on anything by not having a man in her life. But now that he'd been embedded deep inside her, she knew she had been missing out. And she wasn't nearly through making sexy memories with him.

Even as she allowed the fantasy, she reminded herself to draw boundaries around what they were doing together. Not for the sake of her twin sister's reputation, but for her own. Control was important to Hallie—yes, *even* while having fun. She'd simply find a way to do both.

Once her rule-breaking days were over, she could walk away, head held high, with enough sexy memories to fuel her for the rest of her days.

"Place looks good." Gavin's brother Cash walked from one side of the house to the other to admire the views. "You had to outdo me. One waterfront view wasn't enough for you?"

"I wasn't trying for one-upmanship." Gavin handed Cash a beer. "That was a bonus."

Since he'd moved out of his parents' house, Gavin had lived in one apartment after the other. Until recently, when he'd decided to build a home. If asked years ago, he would've sworn he didn't want the hassle of a house. Houses were a lot of work. A ton of responsibility. He liked the idea of renting—of someone else taking care of the inevitable problems that would come up. But lately, with neighbors above, below and on all sides of him—he'd felt boxed in.

He'd be the first to admit a house this size was too much for him. But hell, why not? He worked hard for the money he made, and he had a big extended family. At the rate his brothers were going, Will and Cash and Luke would be populating the Bay with kids in the coming years. Gavin liked the idea of hosting huge family Christmas dinners with his future nieces and nephews. He could be the fun uncle.

In the meantime, he'd settle for using every available surface area as a place to set Hallie before tearing her clothes off and blowing her mind.

"You okay?" Cash interrupted.

"Yeah, why?"

"You're grinning like a moron. Are you reliving the kiss with Hallie Banks, or perhaps what happened after?"

Gavin should have expected that question. He and Hals hadn't exactly made "front-page news," but he'd seen photos of their lip-lock on at least two social media channels. She texted him this morning to assure him he didn't have to worry. She'd evidently talked to Hannah, and neither Hannah nor Will cared what the gossip rags had to say.

"She's the twin sister of a famous person, Gav. That comes with responsibilities." Cash put on his big-brother voice. "There are going to be cameras around. Especially if people think she's Hannah."

"I don't need a lecture." Especially since he was nowhere near ready to share how far he and Hallie had gone last night. There were some details his family didn't need to know.

Cash lifted his beer bottle. "I'm only trying to help."

Even if that was true, it didn't make his brother's interference any less irritating. "So, what, then? I never kiss a woman in public because someone might be watching?"

"We're not talking about any woman. We're talking about Hallie Banks."

"Fine. I'll rephrase. So, I should never kiss *Hallie* in public because someone might be watching and assume she's Hannah?"

"As long as it's okay with Hallie, you can do whatever you want."

And didn't that hearken more memories of last night? She'd been amazingly receptive. Bold and inviting. He'd never forget her perched on his countertop, wearing nothing but his button-down shirt while he fed her ice cream.

"It's more than okay with her, bro. She was the one who attacked me," Gavin said proudly.

"Oh, is that how it happened?" Cash raised a skeptical eyebrow.

"Kind of." Gavin had given her space to come to him, but he'd also encouraged her. He knew what he wanted—*whom* he wanted. When she agreed, he'd counted himself one lucky son of a bitch.

Gavin had been able to think of little else but driving into Hallie's sweet body while she screamed his name. Then she'd mentioned a "next time." He sure as hell hoped she'd been sincere, because he was *in*.

As if he'd summoned her with his mind, his cell phone pinged, her name appearing on his screen. The text read: When's my next lesson?

He wanted to reply *right now*, but he had approximately three thousand things on his to-do list. Damn his overachiever tendencies. He settled for: How's Friday?

Her one-word response came half a second later: Perfect.

Like her, he thought. Then he was jolted from his stupor when his brother smacked his arm harder than necessary to get his attention.

"Shit, brother. You're smiling at your phone like a besotted teenager."

"You'd know," Gav grumbled, uncomfortable. He'd long avoided being "besotted" by anyone. Although, in Hallie's case he'd make an exception. He'd be her sex slave any damn day of the week.

"Well, now you can fill your huge house with babies. After you get married, of course." Cash's grin was pure evil.

"Do *not* start." Especially on the heels of a night filled with hot, sweaty sex in said huge house.

"Eh, I'm busting your balls. Each of us has our own path. You are no exception." Cash rested a hand on Gavin's shoulder. "No matter what you are or are not doing with Hallie Banks, make sure she knows your intentions. You don't want her expecting something from you you're not able to give."

Insulted, Gavin swatted his brother's hand away. "What the hell's that supposed to mean?"

"It *means* her sister is married to your brother. And her best friend is going to be married to me. *And* her other close friend is engaged to Luke. If things advance between you, she might expect a similar outcome."

"Relax. It was just a kiss." Even though what followed couldn't be described as "just" anything. "The lyrics of your love songs are poisoning your brain."

"Don't get your jockstrap in a knot. Just tell her what's up. She is—"

"Hannah's sister. I know, I know." How could he forget with everyone reminding him all the damn time? "But just as I am not you and you are not Luke and Luke is not Will, so Hallie is *not* Hannah. And you know what? Hallie has been taking care of Hannah's career and schedule for years. She is one of the most responsible, intelligent, together women I've met. She can handle me."

And boy, had she.

"I've seen the way she looks at you." Cash took a long swig of his beer and amended, "*Presley* pointed out the way she looks at you. I'm not sure I would have noticed. But Pres, she knows plenty about Hallie and I know plenty about you. I'm trying to steer you away from the rocks."

"You mean in case I *accidentally* get engaged, married and have a few babies before I know what's happened to me?" Gavin gave his brother a half smile, trying not to think too hard about anything he'd just said. Engaged or married would be alarming states to find himself in, but babies? Yikes. For a guy who wasn't looking for a ton of responsibility, a bundle of joy would be anything but.

"Now, that'd be something to see." Cash chuckled.

An involuntary shiver traced Gavin's spine.

"Never say never. I didn't plan to be engaged to be married and talking about babies, either. Look at me now."

"Yeah, living in a less impressive house than your younger brother," Gavin quipped, pleased when Cash stopped grinning. "Come on, I'll show you the rest of my castle."

Cash followed Gavin out the patio door, thankfully leaving talk of marriage and kids behind.

Fourteen

When his doorbell rang Friday night, Gavin didn't expect to find a woman on his doorstep, so the sight of two of them momentarily threw him.

"Hallie," he greeted. "Ruby."

"Hey, Gav." Ruby was smiling as she strode in. "I won't be long. I wanted to drop off my invoice."

"In person, no less." When Hallie would have passed by, too, he snagged her waist, outfitted in a slim black dress, and placed a brief kiss on the center of her lips. "Hi."

"Hi." She blushed prettily, but the moment was interrupted by Ruby's voice calling from the kitchen.

"I was in the neighborhood. Planned on leaving this on your doorstep but then I saw Hallie and I had to say hello." There was a pause and then, "This looks yummy. I'm interrupting."

She was referring to the charcuterie plate and bottle of wine for two Gavin had arranged. Much as he liked Ruby, at the moment, yeah, she was interrupting. Nevertheless, he said, "Thanks for stopping by."

"No problem." Ruby flashed him a knowing smile. "Anyway. I'll be going. Oh, and I appreciate the referral to your friend Mark."

"No problem." He didn't hesitate to refer her to his friends. Ruby was incredible at her job.

Her eyes flitted across the room. "The chair came in!"

"It looks better than I thought," Hallie chimed in, following Ruby into the living room, where they took turns stroking the fabric.

"This is my favorite part—the final walk-through," Ruby told Hallie. "To see how all we've imagined came together. Have you seen the rest yet?"

Hallie bit her lip before admitting, "Only the kitchen."

He remembered the kitchen, too. Their frantic need for each other, the high keening sounds she'd made when she was coming. The ice cream after, and how delicate she'd looked, dressed in naught but his shirt. Yeah, he needed to usher Ruby out of here.

"I'll come back at a more convenient time." Ruby gave Hallie a quick hug.

"I hope I'm here when you do," Hallie told her. "I would be so fascinated to hear your take. You really have an eye." Her face fell the slightest bit, which made him reconsider. Yes, he was anxious to have Hallie to himself, but he would have plenty of time for that later.

"Why not now?" Hands in his pockets, he gave Hallie a small smile.

Ruby's eyes went to the spread in the kitchen and then narrowed on Gavin. "You sure?"

"If it's okay with you." Hallie grinned at Ruby before sending Gavin a pleased smile.

"Of course it's okay with her. She lives for this stuff," he said easily as he crossed to the kitchen island— *not* the one he and Hallie had christened, that one was sacred—and poured two glasses of wine. "I showed Cash around, but I haven't taken a close look. We mostly drank beer and bitched about work." Not entirely true, but he wasn't about to bring up how Cash had cornered him about Hallie and marriage and kids.

He delivered a glass to each of the women in his living room. Gavin's gaze shifted to Hallie, and she nearly took his breath away. He had no clue how he'd confused her for Hannah. They were so different.

"I'm excited to see the bedrooms," Hallie said. Ruby hoisted her eyebrows and Hallie added, "I mean the uh, the um…wall art we talked about in particular."

"Is that what arrived today?" He pointed out a flat cardboard package leaning against the stairs. "I didn't know if I should open it or not."

"Avoidance. I'd expect that from him," Ruby quipped. "Hallie picked it out."

"You'll like it," Hallie promised.

"Let's check out this floor first." Ruby looped her arm in Hallie's and headed for the hallway. Gavin popped a piece of cheese into his mouth, grabbed a bottle of water from the fridge and followed.

Throughout the tour, he learned a lot of things he didn't think he cared about, but Ruby's and Hallie's excitement was weirdly contagious.

Hallie knew his taste and his style. Yes, he'd opened the door for the furniture delivery guys and showed them to the rooms where they'd placed the various pieces of furniture, but until Hallie and Ruby were chattering about the style of the headboard on the guest bed and the reasoning behind choosing an electric lamp that resembled an oil lamp, he hadn't thought too deeply about it.

"They're reminiscent of portals," Hallie said, outlining the circles hewn into the wooden headboard with one finger. "Because you live on the water."

"And the oil lamp is like one on a ship," he guessed.

"Clever, right?" Ruby asked, taking a sip of her wine. "Hallie's idea."

"It's my favorite part of this room," he said. Aside from Hallie being in it.

The tour continued and he found himself paying closer attention to the details. He didn't know how to put what he liked into words, but Hallie did. She seemed to know him as well as, or better than, he knew himself. The furniture was understated and classy. The colors were muted but interesting. And, as she'd promised at dinner last week, each room featured a unique punch of color.

"Okay, Gav." Ruby put her foot on the first step. "Grab your new artwork and bring it upstairs. I want to see it."

"Me, too," he admitted, hefting the large painting in both hands.

The twinkle in Hallie's eye made him wonder if she'd pilfered a nude photo of him and commissioned an artist. He hoped not. Though, if she had, he'd probably find it funny.

"The master bedroom is my favorite space in this house," Ruby said as she stepped into his bedroom. Thankfully his laundry had made it into the basket this morning. He'd cleaned up knowing Hallie was coming over tonight. Though his plans for her in this room were *not* revealing a piece of artwork while Ruby looked on.

Gavin had to agree with her about the space, though. The upstairs bedroom spanned the entire width of the house, with balconies on both sides to take advantage of the dual lake views. The attached master bath featured both a huge soaking tub and a glass-walled shower, and the western-facing balcony was outfitted with a hot tub he hadn't had the pleasure of using yet.

The focal point of his room was the enormous bed, with its tall, black leather headboard punctuated with decorative black rivets. Hallie ran her hand along the bold red bedspread.

"The same color as the car you didn't buy," she said, a teasing lilt in her voice.

His mind went straight to her on his bed, her blond hair a riot of waves around her on a backdrop of red. He'd seen every inch of her naked skin in the bright kitchen lighting, but he was looking forward to dimming the lights in here and stripping her bare. Then they'd try a few new things. Sexy, dastardly things.

"Open your art," Ruby insisted, snapping him out of his fantasy.

He tore the seam in the packaging, laughing when he unveiled what it held. An oversize rendering of a bowl of ice cream, chocolate sauce and caramel and whipped cream like the sundae he'd shared with Hallie. The addition of fresh strawberries matched the vibrant red of the bedspread.

"It's perfect." He cupped Hallie's hip and kissed her cheek. "I'm hanging it over the bed. You can't stop me."

"I can't wait to see it hung," Hallie purred, her long-lashed eyelids closing over her beautiful eyes.

A beat passed and then another before Ruby awkwardly cleared her throat. "I should be going. I forgot I had to pick up…something. From the store."

She gave Hallie a quick hug, patted Gavin's arm and fled the room. She called out, "Goodbye!" from the bottom of the stairs before the wide front door closed with an exaggerated slam.

"Is the meaning behind the ice cream that obvious?" A crease of worry appeared between Hallie's eyebrows.

"Let's hope not." He chuckled as he ran his hand up her back. Leaning to whisper in her ear, he murmured, "I think she picked up on the sparks flying between us."

"I noticed those, too." Hallie tipped her chin and he kissed her, lingering over her delicious lips until she pulled away.

Her hands clutching the front of his shirt, she aimed hazel eyes up at him. "Now what?"

"Like you don't know?" He grinned, happy to have

her here, in his arms, in his house. "Rule-breaking time, sweetheart."

"Skinny-dipping in the hot tub?"

He hummed, pretending to think about it. "That's too tame. But your dare does involve water."

"Uh-oh. Should I be worried?"

"A little. Did you bring a swimsuit?"

"Do I need one?"

"No, ma'am. You definitely don't."

Fifteen

At the mouth of Gavin's garage, Hallie gasped. A bright red—correction: *Candied Apple red*—sports car was parked in its recesses.

"You bought it!"

His expression was proud. "I felt challenged when you said you were surprised I didn't."

"Couldn't part with the truck, I see." The remaining space in the garage held his gray F-150.

"I'm attached." He shrugged. It was so endearing she wanted to melt into him. "I almost confessed when you pointed out the red bedspread reminded you of the car, but I thought it would be more fun to surprise you."

She stroked the hood of the car with her fingertips. He was still smiling, a secret hiding in the depths of his eyes.

"Let's take her for a spin."

"Where are we going?" she asked, trying not to appear overeager.

"Wouldn't you like to know."

She laughed. "I would, actually. Do I need my purse?"

"Sweetheart, you don't need anything. Well, a coat if you want to put the top down."

She ran inside and grabbed her coat, wondering what "rule" he was going to challenge her to break tonight. Was it only driving a topless convertible in December, or would he require her to be topless, too? Or maybe they'd find a private part of the lake and park, and make out hot and heavy in the car. The prospect should have made her nervous, but instead she found it sort of… *thrilling*.

She climbed into the passenger seat, inhaling the fantastic new-car smell. When she opened her eyes and faced her driver, he was smiling at her.

"You are gorgeous tonight, by the way. This dress." His eyes dipped approvingly to the low-cut V in the front of her wrap dress.

"Thank you."

"Don't thank me yet." He backed out of the garage into the driveway and pressed a button. The convertible top unfolded, gifting them a view of a zillion stars sparkling on a blanket of navy blue.

She braced for the brisk ride, but they didn't go far. Mere minutes after she'd snapped her seat belt, he pulled to a stop at the edge of the lake. In the distance, a few boats puttered along. But at the dock, where he parked, there was nothing but trees and a secluded beach.

She was about to congratulate herself on guessing correctly—and tell him that she was surprisingly okay with sex in the car—when he climbed out and opened her door. They walked to the edge of the dock and peered down at the black water.

"Your challenge, Hallie Banks, if you choose to accept it—" he lifted their linked hands and kissed hers "—is to strip to your skivvies and cannonball into the water."

"What!" She laughed, hoping he'd join in and then tell her he was kidding. When he didn't, she said, "You're insane."

"A bit," he admitted with a feral grin. "Not only is the water damn cold, but we're trespassing. This is private property."

She looked over her shoulder at the corner of a house hidden behind a grove of trees. Trespassing broke a *big* rule for her. There could be someone inside, peering through the trees. Or a boat could troll by when she was stripping down and preparing to leap in. Though that was unlikely, given the temperature tonight.

The lake, even cold, was far more appealing in the bright sunshine. Who knew what lurked beneath its black surface? Fish, definitely. Snapping turtles, possibly. An alligator that had been flushed down the toilet and had grown to disturbing proportions? Unlikely, but you never knew.

"Oh, and one more thing," he said, interrupting the horror movie unfolding in her head. "I'll strip down as much as you do."

She propped her hand on her hip. "Down to the skin?"

"If you do it first." He took a look around and she looked with him. A few boats were docked in the distance, most likely empty and too far off to see Hallie or Gavin in the grainy darkness if they weren't. "When we're done here, you can climb into my hot tub and warm up. Because this water is going to be *seriously* cold. If you make me leap in naked, then there will be no hiding what happens if the water's as cold as I expect."

She grinned. She couldn't help it. He was so *fun*. "Then why are you offering to—to—"

"Get naked with you? Are you kidding?" His smile was as sexy as the rest of him. "Freezing or no, naked is always my preference when it comes to you, Hals. And you already know what I'm packing."

Her shoulders shook with laughter. "You are shameless."

"I like to think of myself as confident, but let's say yes on both counts."

At the end of the dock, she considered her options. The good news was she had worn a sturdy bra and a pair of underpants that wouldn't come off when she dived in. On the other hand, if she stripped to the skin, Gavin would be forced to do the same. She loved the idea of calling him on his dare.

His hands landed on her hips, his body warming hers from behind. "You're thinking about it."

"Only because I want to give you a taste of your own medicine."

"Why don't you give me a taste of your lips instead?"

The offer was too good to resist, especially since she hadn't had a real kiss from him in what felt like forever. She turned in the circle of his arms, cupped his neck and lifted her chin. He lowered his mouth and kissed her, teasing the seam of her lips with his tongue before deepening their connection.

The kiss intensified and he hugged her close, his arms locked at her back, a low groan eking from his throat. She kissed him until her breasts were flattened against his chest and their hips bumped with an urgency to do far more than was publicly decent.

But she wasn't going to back out. No matter how badly she wanted him. She'd worried about consequences for far too long. Worried about the effects of her actions on Hannah's life rather than considering their effects on her own.

Hallie took a deliberate step away from him, walking backward on the creaking boards of the dock, and shed her jacket. Brisk air cooled her arms, but she ignored it and untied the belt holding her dress closed. When she opened the fabric and bared her bra and panties to him, she sucked in a breath of pure cold. Goose bumps lit her skin. Gavin's proud, awestruck expression encouraged her to keep going.

She had never skinny-dipped in her life. And now here she was, in complete control *and* having fun. Only Gavin could have convinced her to do something this crazy.

"Challenge accepted, Sutherland." She unhooked her

bra and threw it at his face. He caught it in midair as she
pushed her panties to her ankles and kicked them off.

Steeling herself one last time, she blew out a breath,
turned and leaped into the freezing water.

Gavin had been on the verge of telling her she didn't
have to jump into the lake. Half of him had been push-
ing her for fun, the other half curious how far she'd go.
He'd never expected her to take off all her damn clothes.

She hadn't given him time to argue. One second she
was tongue-wrestling him, the next she was tearing off
her dress like she had no qualms about it whatsoever.
Who was this intriguing woman?

He was still staring into the dark water, her bra in
his hand, when she sputtered to the surface and sucked
in a breath.

Damn. He couldn't believe she'd done it.

"How is it?" he asked with a laugh.

"Not bad." She treaded water, her smile intact. Maybe
he'd miscalculated and the water wasn't as cold as he'd
thought. "What are you waiting for?"

"What I was waiting for already happened," he told
her before tucking her bra into his pocket.

"We had a deal."

"That we did." He wasn't thrilled about it, but he'd
promised. He made quick work of shucking his clothes
and, before he lost his nerve, jumped in.

Holy. *Hell.*

The water hit him like ice. He combed through
the frigid lake to burst to the surface, gasping when
his head popped out of the water. He was greeted by

Hallie's laughter...followed by the audible chattering of her teeth.

"Are you kidding me?" His voice was higher than he would've liked. His balls had shrunk to the size of sugar peas.

"Hey, this was your idea."

"I didn't know it'd be *this* cold."

"I'm less afraid of the cold and more afraid of giant alligators."

"A giant alligator would have the sense to stay out of frigid water."

She glided closer, brushing his shoulder with her arm, or possibly her breast. He couldn't tell. The water hadn't become warmer, but his bloodstream sure had. Her small hands came to rest on his shoulders and he guided her legs around his waist, swimming to a shallow part where he could put his feet on the sandy bottom.

"I'm suddenly much warmer," he lied, swiping away a droplet of water as it trickled down her nose.

"Same." She tipped her head and kissed him.

"Your lips are turning blue. You were crazy to take me up on this."

"What can I say? Whenever I'm around you, I do crazy things."

"I'm not gonna lie, I like that about you." He wrapped his arms around her back and held her close. "You deserve to have some fun."

"What else do I deserve?" Her legs wrapped at his waist, she rubbed her center against his budding erection. *Amazing.* Even in cold water she could bring him to life. Every part of him—especially one part—wanted to lose himself in her heat. But he forced himself to wait. There would be later. When they were both a hell of a lot warmer.

"You know," she said, absently toying with his wet hair, "when I asked you to help me with this rule-breaking thing, I didn't expect to be naked with you in Mountain View Lake. But now that I am…" She surprised the hell out of him by grinding her hips against his. Now parts of her and parts of him were brushing against each other, the murky water between them icy cold and sharp, yet soft at the same time. "How do you feel about breaking in your brand-new bed?"

"Fantastic." Unbidden, his brother's warning about letting her know exactly what Gavin was thinking came out of nowhere and rang in his ears. He wasn't sure when the best time would be to bring it up, but hell, why not now? "Hallie… We should probably talk about your expectations."

"Okay," she said pragmatically. "I expect an orgasm. Two, if you can manage."

He choked on a laugh as his own teeth began to chatter. "If you recall, you had *two* the other night."

"Yes, but that could have been dumb luck. I also expect these rule-breaking experiments to continue a while longer. At least until I'm accustomed to breaking them. And—" she held up a finger to punctuate her point "—I want to try the hot tub. I deserve it now that I've been forced to skinny-dip in this freezing lake."

Damn, he liked when she was confident. Take-charge. *Willing.* She'd thoroughly shaken off her timidity with him. No matter what happened when this was over, he'd be the one who'd helped Hallie Banks break out of her shell.

When his thoughts devolved to how things might end between them, he shook them off—not hard to do while suffering from hypothermia. She liked him and he liked her a whole hell of a lot. He rerouted his focus on the challenge she'd issued.

"Shimmy your cute ass up the ladder and grab your clothes," he told her. "And then you and I will see about those orgasms."

Sixteen

They climbed out of the freezing lake water, gathered their clothes and dressed quickly. The short drive back to his house seemed to take an eternity. And not only because he worried they might freeze to death before they made it to his house.

"I'm beginning to understand that your lack of fun-having," he said, angling the vent to blow warm air on her, "has less to do with your not knowing how to do it and more to do with you needing control over every situation. You're a natural rule-breaker, Hals."

"I never would have thought so until now." She snuggled deep in her coat. "But I think you're right. I've been in control for so long, it's hard to let go."

"Especially when you know handing it off could result in disaster." He pulled into his driveway and opened the garage door. He understood the disaster part all too well. His job was to be in control. He wrangled out-of-control situations—or ones that could spiral out of control—into some semblance of order.

"The rub is if you screw up, you're the only one to blame."

"Been there." Nothing was worse than failing. Or expending well-meaning effort and then landing face-first in the dirt. The thought came that he'd played it safe in some areas of his life to avoid failure, but he shrugged the idea off. He wasn't going to waste a single second with Hallie turning *that* over in his head.

"So we both like control. How's this going to work?" He killed the engine and punched the button on a remote, bringing the garage door down. "You caught me off guard at the lake, but when it comes to you and me taking this inside, and upstairs, and into the hot tub…" A slow grin spread his lips as he imagined the ways he would have her. "Who calls the shots?"

Her eyes sparkled. She was enjoying herself as much as he was. "We can take turns."

"Hell yeah, we can." He would have his way with her, but he also liked the idea of her having her way with him.

Inside, they kicked off their soggy shoes and walked over to the kitchen counter. The cheese platter had been sitting out too long to appear appetizing, but the wine was still good.

"Can I pour you a drink?"

"It's not necessary."

"I didn't say it was necessary." He grabbed a pair of

fresh wineglasses and poured. "If nothing else, this will warm you up." Her hair was wet and wavy, the strands curling on the ends.

She sipped the wine, her eyes closing as she savored it. God, she was beautiful. How did he get so lucky?

"You're right. This is warming me up a little." She put the glass down and licked her lips almost nervously. "I need to be honest with you about something. You don't have to try this hard. The bar for romance is set pretty low for me."

He didn't like hearing that. He set his glass next to hers. "Meaning?"

"Meaning—" she shrugged one shoulder "—the places I have been 'romanced' aren't exactly romantic. There was that time in the car..."

"Ah, yes. The requisite car sex," he interjected. "Overeager first time?"

"You guessed it. The second time was on the couch."

He winced and guessed, "Parents' basement?"

"His. Not Gram's basement. She would've killed me."

He had to chuckle. He could only imagine Eleanor Banks's reaction if she'd found Hallie attempting intercourse on the family's floral couch. Her gram would have chased the boy out of her house with a shotgun. "I'm not laughing at you, more at how similar our situations have been. It's tragic the shit we do when we're young. We're in such a hurry, we miss out on the good stuff."

"I'm not sure I ever made it to the good stuff. Until you, I mean."

Now, that was sweet. She'd just unwittingly set the tone for tonight. "New plan. I'm gonna give you a night you'll remember for the rest of your life. You shouldn't settle for less than you deserve, Hals."

Her eyes warmed like he'd touched a deep part of her.

"Why don't you call the shots tonight?" he offered, taking up his wineglass again. "Use me up. Think you can handle me?"

She answered by smoothing her hands down his shirt and then unbuckling his belt. By the time her golden eyes peered up at him he was damn near breathless.

"I take that as a *yes*," he wheezed.

"Definitely a *yes*," she confirmed. "We can start with a shower."

The smell of citrus and pine soap infiltrated her senses as her mind blanked of thought.

His hands were on her breasts, his soapy fingers plucking at her nipples. Warmth gathered between her legs as she squirmed against the smooth tile wall of the shower, her mouth open to let out a moan of pure bliss.

That time in the car, the time on the couch in the basement and the handful of other forgettable times she'd been intimate with her exes faded into the ether the second Gavin guided her under one of the sprayers and slipped his fingers between her legs.

He stroked her while kissing her deeply, his facial hair scraping her mouth, his seeking tongue hot on hers. Then he left her so abruptly, she had to put her hands out to keep from sliding down the wall.

She blinked down at him, on his knees before her in

the huge shower. Water trickled down his cheeks, droplets bouncing off his head. His hands were wrapped around her thighs and he instructed her to come closer, using deliciously dirty words to do it.

A second later, he put his tongue to better use and lapped at her folds. She did what came naturally, which was rest her hands on his head and run her fingers through his damp hair.

Her hips thrust. She rode his tongue as he delivered blow by blow to her most intimate part. As she was coming apart, her legs shaking beneath his hands, he slipped a finger into her, and then two.

A long groan of pleasure—hers—echoed off the shower walls. The orgasm hit her with a rush, stars appearing on the screens of her eyelids. She rested the back of her head against the shower wall. By the time her breathing had regulated and his hands had returned to her thighs, she realized she was gripping his hair with enough force to pull it from the roots.

"Oh my God." She released him. "I'm sorry. I'm so sorry." Her voice was a puny rasp, her apology as limp as her limbs.

He rose to his feet slowly and her eyes feasted on his body. His muscular chest with the perfect amount of chest hair, the bumps of his abs, the sharp delineations next to his hip bones. She'd never tire of seeing him naked—she thought she'd committed the vision to memory, but here she was ogling him like it was the first time.

"Never," he warned, his face devoid of his usual smile. "Never apologize for coming on my tongue."

She blushed furiously and then his grin appeared.

"What's next on your wish list? More of the same?" He palmed her throbbing sex and she shuddered. "I can go all night if you like."

"You're too much." She bit her lip. He thumbed the tender flesh away from her teeth and kissed her.

"I'm exactly what you ordered. So, start ordering."

Carte blanche access to Gavin Sutherland. Where to begin? But she knew. It's what she'd been wanting for as long as she could remember.

"The bed."

"Traditional," he said before he spun the shower knobs to turn off the water. "But I'll allow it."

He dried off quickly, swiping her towel from her before she could finish drying herself. Water ran down her legs and back as his mouth collided with hers.

"I'm wet," she breathed as he backed her toward the bed.

"I know," he growled.

Then she was falling back onto the bed and he was over her, every inch of his yummy, muscled body blanketing hers. They'd warmed up quickly in the shower after skinny-dipping. She'd noticed his um, *member*, had recovered nicely. She palmed his thick erection, enjoying both heft and length.

He sucked a breath through his teeth.

"Condoms are in the nightstand." He kissed her long and slow. "Unless you want to do it bareback again."

"Bareback is best," she admitted. "I trust you."

"I trust you, too."

She felt safe with him, but knowing he felt safe with her bolstered her confidence.

He placed a kiss on each of her breasts and positioned himself between her legs. Beneath him, she marveled at his delicious male form. How many times had she averted her gaze or turned her attention elsewhere over the years, not wanting him to know she'd been watching him? What a waste. There was so much of him to admire, and she could have been admiring him openly.

One smooth tilt of his hips and he was sliding deep. She guided him, her heels digging into his very fine ass, her head thrown back in ecstasy. His mouth landed on her neck, where he suckled her pulse and began to move. She took him easily, primed and ready thanks to the intimate kisses in the shower.

This was great sex. The other night hadn't been a fluke—which she'd known, of course. Sex this good was why sonnets were written and why love songs were crooned. She imagined sex this good was also why breakups hurt like physical wounds, why exes got back together. Interesting how sex could cause either undying devotion or irreparable devastation.

He gripped her hand, laced their fingers together and lifted her arm over her head. Then he grabbed her other hand and joined it with the first one.

"Is this okay?" He drove deep and sent a ripple of pleasure through her entire body.

"Yes, Gavin. *Yes*."

Everything he did was a *yes*. From slow strokes that wound her tighter and tighter, to the faster, pistoning pace that had her screaming his name.

She reveled in every second of being with him—from the kisses he placed on her throat to his teeth nipping her earlobe. Another orgasm crashed over her, pulling her beneath the surface. He released her hands to hold himself up as his frantic pace continued. She wrapped her arms and legs around him and took what he gave, her entire body shaking with pleasure.

He shouted his release, his deep groans lost in her hair. She encouraged him to give her his weight. He did, his body hot and damp on hers. His breaths audible against her ear.

Peace settled over her—over both of them. She had never experienced sex this powerful before. She warned herself not to read too much into it until he raised his head to study her. His stunned expression said it all.

Whatever had just happened between them wasn't commonplace for him, either.

Which meant this was either the best thing that had ever happened to them, or a catastrophe of the worst magnitude.

It was too soon to tell.

Seventeen

At Elite, Hallie walked in expecting anything. Hannah and Will were still in France but planning on returning at the end of the week. Gavin was the one who had asked Hallie to come in, stating he had a surprise for her.

Considering his surprises ranged from fun to freezing, she had no idea what he would spring on her today.

In the empty hallway, her heels clicked on the floor. She had worn her favorite black pantsuit with a daring pair of sexy shoes. She thought Gavin would appreciate them.

As she approached the conference room, he stepped out of the doorway and scooped her against him. Before she knew what was happening, his lips were on hers. She hummed against his mouth, reveling in his solid warmth and the feeling of being held.

He pulled away, ending their lip-lock with a soft smooching sound. "Hello, gorgeous."

Seriously, how great was he? "I assume no one's here."

"Just me and you."

"I want to make it perfectly clear that I'm all for breaking rules, but I doubt your oldest brother would appreciate us having sex on his recording studio's conference room table."

Gavin's eyebrows climbed his forehead. "Not what I was going to suggest, dirty girl. But now that you mention it…"

He dropped a fast kiss on her mouth when she giggled.

It'd been a week-plus of bliss with him. She'd gone to his house several times for dinner followed by dessert, or followed by sex and *then* dessert. Last night, he'd stayed over at her place after all three.

"How is it that I left your bed hours ago and already miss this body?" His hands bracketing her hips, he tugged her close and dropped his forehead on hers.

"Because we're really, really good at turning each other on." She'd gone from barely being able to look at him to boldly meeting his eyes and flirting. She loved the change. She was also fairly certain she could easily fall in love with him if she didn't proceed very carefully. Funny how the challenge to be less careful also required her to be more careful. No matter how much fun they had, she'd do well to remember Gavin was a consummate bachelor. It was best to keep things simple.

"Thanks for meeting me here. I have a million things

to do or I would have come to you. In fact—" he glanced down at a shiny gold wristwatch "—I have a conference call in five minutes. Sorry to rush you."

"No, it's fine. I was on my way to a coffee date with Pres anyway."

"Perfect. You can ask her opinion about this." He pushed the conference room's door wide and walked her into the room. It took her a hot second to accept what she was seeing.

A bold red sheath dress hung on a hanger from a hook on the wall. The skirt was cut high on one hip and delicate diamond-like stones were sprinkled like stardust along the train.

She floated over, rubbing the satiny fabric between her fingertips.

"Do you like it?" he asked.

"No," she breathed, smiling over her shoulder at him. "I *love* it."

His smile was pleased. "You scared me for a second. Hannah picked it out. I called and asked her for help with a dress for Mags Dumond's Winter Party. And since red is our color…"

"We have a color?" Yep, she was going to dissolve into a puddle at his feet.

"Guess so. You deserve a dress of your own, Hals. Not a hand-me-down from your sister."

"Yes, it would be a shame to wear vintage couture Valentino," she teased.

"Will you be my date?"

"To Mags's party?" A photo on the internet was one thing, but an intimate party where their families would be in attendance… "Are you sure that's a good idea? Everyone will be there."

"Another rule to break. A very public date to one of the biggest gatherings in Beaumont Bay. You'll be with me and everyone will know it."

Maybe she hadn't been wrong about the earth moving beneath them. Clearly, he'd felt it, too. "Are you sure that's okay with you?"

He pulled her close. "Do you think I would've had this dress special made and shipped from Paris, France, if I wasn't positive I wanted you to be seen with me?"

"This is a very, very good surprise." She touched his cheek and he lowered his mouth to hers for another kiss. "Much better than skinny-dipping in the freezing lake."

"Never going to let me live that down, are you?"

"No, I don't think I will." *Never* was a long time, and part of her wanted to ask if he was considering a future with her. Even though she'd just sternly reminded herself they didn't have one, she wouldn't deny that part of her wanted it. Every moment they spent together was better than the last.

Could she convince him to leave behind the reasons he had for not settling down? Or had their time together changed his mind already? He'd been enjoying watching her come out of her shell, and she had him to thank for embracing her bolder, more colorful side. They were growing and, to her at least, it looked like they were growing in the same direction.

His phone beeped. He shot her a regretful frown as he reached for it. "That's my alarm. I have to hop on a call."

"It's fine. Really." It would be best to leave before she said any of the thoughts jumbled up in her head aloud. "Thank you for the dress."

"You're welcome." He plucked the hanger and draped the dress over her arms before kissing her goodbye. "I'll stop by your place tonight. I'll help you pick out what to wear under the dress."

She practically floated out of the building while admiring the gown in her arms. She would be stepping out in style come Saturday. *With Gavin.* Which, fine, okay, was a little scary, but it was also exciting. Maybe she'd been wrong to think holding back was the answer.

Why not move forward instead?

Gavin showed up as promised and, as expected, was making out with her on the couch within thirty seconds of him walking through the door. That escalated to kissing in the bedroom, which had escalated to sex. Hallie was learning fantastic sex with him was not a rarity—he was always phenomenal.

"If we keep this up, I'm going to be able to skip a lot more workouts." Gavin, on his back, one arm thrown over his head, looked like every erotic fantasy she'd never dared having. He was gloriously naked, his rugged masculinity offset by her pale pink sheets.

"You weren't the only one working up a sweat." She was proud of her participation in this evening's sex-a-thon. She'd been on top, riding him for a good long while. She smoothed her hand over his soft chest hair before stroking the growth on his jaw. "Did you always have this?"

"You mean after puberty, I assume?"

"*Yes*, that's what I mean. I can't imagine you with a smooth face. It doesn't suit you."

"I don't know if a smooth face suits me or not, but it does make me look about ten years younger. And in court you don't want to look any younger. Unless you're trying to pass as a minor."

She propped her head on one hand, the other resting on his stomach. "I find it so interesting that you became a lawyer, since you're the only one in your family."

"My uncle is a lawyer. Criminal defense." He rested his hand over hers. "Distant uncle."

"You have to wonder what kind of family traits are passed on from an uncle who's a criminal defense lawyer. What did you inherit?"

"Well, he married into the Sutherland family, so I don't think he counts. Speaking of family, there was a question I wanted to ask you."

She liked hearing he'd been thinking of her. Knowing she'd been on his mind when they weren't together like he was on hers most of the time. "You have my attention."

"How many sets of twins are in your family?"

"Several, actually. My cousins are twin boys, identical. And my grandmother and my great-aunt are identical twins."

"Not Eleanor," he guessed correctly.

"No. This would be my dad's mom. Oh, and I think there was a recent set of fraternal twins born on his side, as well, but I haven't met them."

"A lot of twins."

"Our parents knew to stop at one set. You're from a fairly large family. Four children isn't a small number. And your mom didn't do two in one go the way my mom did. She had you one at a time."

"The old-fashioned way," he joked, and she smiled.

"How many kids do you want to have?"

"No, no, no." He shook his head.

"I assume by that answer the number is zero?"

"I have no plans to settle down. A family is a lot of responsibility."

"So is a house." She kept her smile but was surprised by his extreme reaction. She'd always envisioned herself married with children. One child, at least. Though she'd certainly accept two if the twin gene came through.

"In case you haven't noticed…" He rolled over and faced her, propping his own head in his hand. "I'm a stuck-in-his-ways bachelor. Kids are great. Families are great. For someone else."

"That's fair," she said, meaning it. If she thought about it for longer than five seconds, she could admit she was a stuck-in-her-ways bachelorette. She liked her life the way it was, more now that she'd been shedding her more serious side in favor of cutting loose. She was enjoying the fun side Gavin had helped her uncover.

"But I surprised you."

"A little, but only because you're from a large family. Your brothers have settled into relationships one by one. I assume babies are forthcoming."

"Now who's assuming I'm like my brothers? You, of all people, should know better," he teasingly scolded.

"Oh, no. I did do that." She rolled onto her back and

covered her face with both hands. When she peeked through her fingers, he was hovering over her, his handsome face taking up most of her vision. Which was fine with her, since he was lovely to look at. He tugged her hands from her face.

"I like what we're doing and how we're doing it. Do you?"

"I do. I really do." She heard the unspoken *but*, and he must have, too. He raised his eyebrows and waited for her to continue. "Are you sure Saturday night's party isn't going to change who we are?" Their overly involved families would draw their own conclusions. Or worse, have unrealistic expectations.

"People can say or think whatever they want, but it doesn't have to change what we do. Didn't we learn that when we were making out on the boardwalk?"

"Touché."

He leaned down and kissed her. As his mouth moved along hers, she wondered if he was right. Maybe their future didn't have to look like anyone else's. Maybe her own desire to expect more from him was a habit, rather than what she actually wanted.

He couldn't have laid out what he wanted any clearer, but what he wanted included her. And wasn't having him in her bed enough for the foreseeable future? She'd embraced her new spontaneous side to great success. Why ruin it by trying to exert expectations and control on a situation working out well for both of them?

It didn't matter what their siblings said, or what the town said. What anybody said, really. What Hallie and

Gavin were doing worked for them, and that's what mattered.

His mouth moved from her neck to her breasts and continued a lazy path down her body. He had a way of making her forget about anything but the present, and as far as she was concerned, the present didn't get any better than this.

Eighteen

The night of Mags Dumond's Winter Party came fast.

Normally, Hallie would be preparing to segue every conversation to business, or to her twin sister. The idea of a spotlight on her was overwhelming, which might explain the case of nerves as well as her lack of appetite.

There would truly be nowhere for her to hide tonight. Once she and Gavin entered the party hand in hand, him dashing in his black tuxedo and her glowing like a red beacon, all eyes would be on them.

Since the night in her bed, when she and Gavin agreed they were fine, *thank you very much*, she'd convinced herself she didn't care what anyone thought of their relationship. But her hard-won confidence had been gradually chipping away. While she showered this morning, dressed this afternoon and, now, as they crested the hill atop which sat Mags's mansion.

She squeezed her hands together tightly as he revved the engine. They climbed the driveway in his shiny, outrageous Candied Apple red sports car. She shook her head helplessly. There was no way they'd blend in tonight.

As if he sensed her nerves, his hand landed on top of both of hers. "You're going to do great."

"Easy for you to say. You're not stepping out like Cinderella at the ball."

"From what I recall," he said as he pulled up to the valet stand, "things turned out well for her at the end."

She sent him an impatient glare, but he only grinned.

"Hals. We've been to Mags's mansion a million times."

True. Mags had thrown her own birthday parties, black-and-white balls, costume parties and dinner parties. Tonight's shindig was an evening of cocktails and snacks with a band. Without rigid structure, there would be lots of mingling and free time, which might have been what worried Hallie the most. She didn't mind talking shop or chatting up prospective clients, but she wasn't comfortable when *she* was the topic.

"Maybe no one will notice me," she said, hoping against hope she'd been overreacting.

"Sweetheart." He unbuckled his seat belt and then hers, sliding a seductive gaze down her dress. "Everyone is going to notice you."

Her stomach tightened and then fluttered. A perfect

illustration of how he affected her. He both riled her up and put her at ease.

Her feelings for him had grown and matured from the crush she'd had on him before. Now he was a real, layered man who shared stories with her in bed at night and nuzzled her neck in the kitchen in the morning. He had doubts and hated failing. And even though he'd die before he'd admit it, she knew the idea of a future with her—with anyone—was less about him losing control and more about fearing what the future might bring. The thing was, she understood. Hell, she could relate. She wasn't quite ready for *forever and ever, amen*, either.

Not that her heart had listened to a single of her head's warnings. She fell a little more for him now, in spite of the lectures she'd given herself not to involve her heart in what they were doing.

Enough. No more overthinking tonight. She didn't need the added pressure.

He placed his Stetson on his head and then they walked into Mags's immaculate mansion overlooking the lake—a palace, really—and into a sea of well-dressed people. To Hallie's relief, she spotted a few other red dresses. Although none of them sparkled or had a train, at least she wouldn't be the only woman in red at the party.

Hannah, having recently returned home from France, approached in a pale pink dress. She grasped Hallie's shoulders, holding her at arm's length. "I knew it. I knew it. I knew you'd look scrumptious in this gown."

Gavin, at Hallie's side, shook his brother Will's hand

and accepted a kiss on the cheek from Hannah. She gave him a playful shove and said, "You lucky guy."

"You don't have to tell me twice." He curled an arm around Hallie's shoulders and pressed a kiss to her temple. Hannah and Will didn't appear alarmed. Neither did the people milling around the party turn and gawp. Maybe Hallie had been overreacting.

"Champagne?" Hannah offered.

"Yes, please." Hallie nodded, hoping the bubbles would settle her nervous stomach.

Gavin enjoyed hanging out with Hallie. And only partly because most of their dates ended with exquisite sex. The other night when she'd fallen asleep in his arms, he'd held her close and stared at the ceiling, feeling grateful for the time they'd had together. To think he once believed she'd hated him. They'd come a long way.

He'd issued the challenge tonight for one reason. She was in the habit of putting herself in second place. Of comparing herself with the women around her. Especially Hannah. Hannah didn't try to take the spotlight; it was more like Hallie *gave* it to her.

He wanted Hallie to step into her own spotlight. To be noticed and revered for who she was, rather than who she was related to.

Some of that insight was thanks to his own past experiences. He'd been in the shadows of his three older brothers for a while, and at one point had felt separate from them. Especially when he'd gone to law school instead of into the music business. Sure, he'd parlayed his degree into a music-themed career, but at the time he might as well have been on a different planet from the rest of them.

Once he'd honed his skills and his calling, he'd carved a niche for himself and became wildly successful. Confidence had been a by-product. He wanted the same experience for Hallie. She deserved wild success, too, and the easy confidence that came with knowing she was in exactly the right place.

"Well, if it isn't my beautiful granddaughters." Eleanor Banks embraced Hallie and Hannah, showing no preferential treatment. To Gavin, she offered a lingering gaze he couldn't read at all. "You and Hallie are getting on well."

Since Hallie was standing very close to him, it would be ridiculous to try to pretend he didn't know what Eleanor was talking about.

He slipped his arm around his date's waist and squeezed her close. "She's an incredible woman."

Eleanor smiled. "You're slow on the uptake, but I'll give you credit for finally realizing it."

"Gram," Hallie scolded.

"What? I've always known how special my girls are." With so much confidence ebbing off the Banks family matriarch, there was no way Hallie hadn't inherited some of it.

"Boyfriends are overrated, but they do complement ball gowns nicely," Eleanor added with a wink to Gavin. "Come on, girls, I want to introduce you around, and hopefully avoid that horrible Mags as long as possible."

She ushered Hallie and Hannah away, and Gavin felt sweat prickle his brow beneath his hatband. Not at the mention of Mags—though she was far from his favorite person in this town—but at the word *boyfriend*.

"You need a refill?" Will asked. "Or a toilet? You look green."

Gavin lifted his Stetson and swiped his forehead. "I'm fine."

"This is new for you. Expect an adjustment period."

"I am parched now that you mention it." Gavin downed the few inches of booze at the bottom of his glass.

Will followed him to the bar, where they bumped into Cash and Presley and Luke and Cassandra, who had arrived as a foursome. Cassandra and Presley accepted flutes of champagne and took off in the direction where Hallie and Hannah and Eleanor had vanished. Gavin ordered another bourbon. He felt his brothers' eyes on him as if he'd accidentally worn a tutu instead of a tux.

"What's wrong with him?" Luke asked Will.

"Eleanor Banks referred to him as Hallie's boyfriend."

"Ah," Luke and Cash said in tandem.

Gavin rolled his eyes. "Nothing's wrong with me."

"It's weird, but you'll get used to it," Luke said. "And then you'll be engaged."

"Or married," Will chimed in.

"That's not—" Gavin blew out a breath and opted not to finish that sentence. He wouldn't get far with these three hounding him. "Hallie's great."

"Being part of a couple carries weight," Will said,

not making Gavin feel any better. "You're not used to it, is all. And her sister's incredibly famous."

"I told him that," Cash said.

"*You're* famous," Gavin reminded Cash, his patience ebbing. "I'm used to you."

"It's different when you're with a famous person," Will said, piling on. "You're going to have to set aside your inflated male ego. Wherever you are with her, she'll draw more attention than you."

"You speak from experience?" Gavin snapped.

"Yeah," Will said simply.

"I *want* Hallie to be noticed. Why do you think I bought her that dress?" Gavin asked too loudly. He lowered his voice. "She's a shark when it comes to business. It's time she was recognized for how wonderful she is and not for her proximity to her famous twin sister."

"Uh-oh," Luke murmured. "Worse than we thought."

"No kidding." Cash raised an eyebrow.

Gavin glared at his brothers and was met with matching pitying expressions.

Will slapped Gav's shoulder a little too hard. "Hey, I wanted to talk to you guys about this B and B we stayed in. You have to take your girls to France."

Gavin recognized a purposeful turn of topic when he heard one, but he didn't dare steer the conversation back to him and Hallie. He had a feeling his brothers were hinting that he was further in with her than he was aware.

They were wrong.

He'd taken Cash's advice about being up front with Hallie. When she'd asked about family, he'd laid out how content he was with his bachelor status. She'd been okay with it. Right?

He rubbed the center of his chest, uncomfortable for some reason. Glancing down at his glass, he decided to blame the bourbon.

He wasn't going to let his brothers get in his head any more than they already had. He and Hallie were good. Just the way they were.

Nineteen

"I've never seen you look more stunning!" Cassandra embraced Hallie in another hug. The brunette's big smile and boisterous attitude were completely contagious. Hallie felt shy accepting the compliment. But she tried anyway.

"Thank you." She smoothed her hand along the red sheath. "I feel beautiful wearing it."

"Gavin can't tear his eyes off you," Presley commented.

"That's my favorite part," Hannah said, her gaze following Presley's across the room to where the Sutherland brothers were clustered at the bar. "Hallie has been looking at him like that for years. It's past time he returned the favor."

"Is that true?" Cassandra asked.

"Completely true," Presley said. "She avoided him like crazy when I met her."

"No, I didn't," Hallie murmured. A lie. She had totally avoided him.

Presley's smirk communicated her disbelief. "I'm assuming we're going to see a lot more of you two together."

"Yeah, no more hiding him away in your dark bedroom," Cassandra teased.

"We're just having fun," she reminded them. "Gavin and I are comfortable with the way things are."

"Gram called him your *boyfriend*." Hannah sang the word.

"Gram is a wishful thinker." Hallie raised one eyebrow.

Publicly dating Gavin was one thing, but his being her "boyfriend" was another. There was a traditional, old-school part of her that embraced the idea, but she was now fun-and-fresh Hallie. The other part of her would have to catch up.

"The rule-breaking challenge was the best thing that ever happened to you," Presley said. "You're so happy you're sparkling."

"I think that's the diamonds," Hallie said, swishing her train. She had to smile. She *was* happy. Breaking a few of her rules had changed her life for the better. Was it so outrageous to believe Gavin was benefiting, too? Would he eventually decide he wasn't a stuck-in-his-ways bachelor? Decide that, like his brothers, he was also eager to settle down?

No matter how many times she warned herself to halt

this line of thinking, she couldn't help circling the possibilities. She didn't share her thoughts with her friends or her sister. Instead she sipped champagne and chatted about other innocuous topics. And when Gavin interrupted to ask her to dance, she didn't share her thoughts with him, either.

She simply enjoyed dancing with him, swaying to the music as her gorgeous red dress sparkled under the lights. She kept her eyes on the sprig of holly pinned to his lapel and mused how he looked like a prince. Well, a prince in a cowboy hat, but that worked for her. They enjoyed hors d'oeuvres and she sipped more champagne, laughing and enjoying herself.

By midnight, the party was nowhere near winding down. Hallie, though, had almost had enough "peopling" for one evening. She hid a yawn behind her hand as Gavin made his way back to the bar for a refill. He didn't make it before being corralled into a group of guys she didn't recognize. They were slapping him on the back and laughing. He sent her an apologetic smile, but she waved him off. She needed a breather anyway.

She slipped into a shadowed corner and propped her arms on a high-top table. No one was around, giving her a precious moment to herself. Parties zapped nearly all of her energy. Plus, she wasn't exactly a night owl. She preferred a hot tea over a martini most nights, and that's if she wasn't already asleep by now.

"My goodness, I thought you were Hannah."

Mags Dumond intruded, her hand wrapped around an elegant stemmed glass. Her fingernails were long, painted glittery silver to match her dress. The sequins dotting the fabric were almost holographic. She closely resembled the disco ball hanging over the dance floor.

"Hannah is wearing pink tonight," Hallie said with a patient smile.

"She's also been wearing Will Sutherland. We get it. You're in love." Mags snorted at her own joke before drinking the remainder of her champagne in one gulp. "I noticed you hanging on to a different Sutherland man tonight. You and Gavin on the dance floor." She fanned her face. "Save some for the bedroom!"

Hallie tried to keep the smile pasted on her face, which was always a challenge when dealing with Mags. The older woman had something snarky to say about someone—about *everyone*—if you talked to her long enough.

"What an odd couple you two make."

Case in point.

"Well, it works for us." Hallie was tired, and a little grouchy. She didn't have the stamina to deal with Mags tonight. Hell, she hardly had the stamina to deal with Mags on *any* night. Not that that deterred the party's host.

"Gavin is so… What word am I looking for? *Free-spirited.* He is the least serious of the Sutherland clan. And you, honey, in case you haven't noticed, are no Hannah Banks. You are positively rigid. I can make out the set of your stiff spine in your flowy gown. Ha! I mean, even your irritating grandmother knows how to have fun. You know I'm kidding. I love her," Mags lied with a smile. "Why are you hiding over here in the corner?"

"I'm not hiding," Hallie said through her teeth. She

didn't love personal confrontations, and Mags had made this terribly personal. "Gram is the best person I know."

Unlike Mags. The woman might be rich in dollars, but when it came to kindness she was flat broke.

"Well, of course you think so. Eleanor was the one who took you in after your parents gallivanted off to another part of the world. I've always thought it would be wonderful to do whatever you wanted in life without worrying about consequences. If that's what you're doing with Gavin, honey, my blessings." She waved a taloned hand. "Be careful, though. Consequences have a way of sneaking up on you when you least expect them."

Hallie's face grew hot as a dozen retorts piled up in her throat. Thankfully Gavin approached at that moment, two glasses in his hands.

"There he is! The life of the party. I'm glad to see you with a refill for this one." Mags shot a thumb in Hallie's direction. "She's falling asleep. Liven her up."

With that, she returned to her party, loudly commenting to someone as she went, and likely ruining their day, as well.

"I see she hasn't changed a bit," Gavin said with a headshake. "When is she going to realize that being famous and being infamous aren't the same thing?"

He handed Hallie a glass of champagne and she swallowed a hearty gulp.

"You didn't take whatever she said to heart, I hope." He touched Hallie's shoulder, concern evident on his face.

Tears burned the backs of her eyes. "You didn't hear everything she said."

"I can imagine. Every word rolling off her forked tongue is thoughtless and mean."

True. Mags probably hadn't given much thought to the things she said. But what she'd said to Hallie held an undeniable nugget of truth. Hallie's parents *had* gallivanted off to another part of the world, leaving Hannah and Hallie to be raised by Eleanor. And Gavin *was* the life of the party.

Who did Hallie think she was, trying to convince herself she was a fun, rule-breaking maven? Had she been trying on a new personality, like the red gown, to see if it fit? Mags had seen through Hallie easily. Hallie knew deep down she and Gavin were an odd couple, which was why Mags's pointing it out hurt so much.

If it was obvious to Mags that Gavin and Hallie didn't belong together, it was probably obvious to a lot of other people, too. For all her shortcomings, Mags Dumond had told Hallie the truth. Hallie knew she wasn't supposed to care what other people thought, but part of her did. She and Gavin were cut from two very different cloths—his vibrant red, and hers boring beige. She had been playing a part by wearing this dress and showing up on his arm tonight. Who did she think she was trying to pass herself off as carefree?

"I'm tired," she said, and wasn't that the truth. She was absolutely beat.

"Okay, well, we can leave." Her handsome, accommodating date cupped her elbow with one hand. "If you're sure you're ready."

"I'm sure. It's been a long day and this party has been

particularly draining. I've talked about myself enough to last two lifetimes."

They said quick goodbyes to her sister and friends and his brothers. Thankfully, no one guilted them into staying for one more drink. Once they were on the road, Gavin turned toward his own house instead of hers.

"Where are we going?"

"My place. I have a hot tub with your name on it."

"I'm better off alone." She hated how true that sounded. She was used to being alone, to handling emotional pitfalls by herself. As much as she wanted to lean on him, it seemed foolish to get used to his being around.

"I respect that, Hals, I do. But you can be alone at my house. I'm not taking you home when you don't feel well. I hate the idea of you there without me."

"That's…actually really thoughtful," she admitted.

He gripped her hand. "Don't start that rumor, whatever you do. You'll ruin my cutthroat-lawyer reputation."

She was too tired to laugh, but she did spare him a smile. He wasn't the problem tonight. Maybe she had taken what Mags said personally. Maybe she'd wake after a good night's sleep in Gavin's arms and feel completely refreshed.

Back at his house, they stripped out of their evening attire and stepped onto the balcony overlooking the private lake. The wind was crisp, but the water in the hot tub was warm and silky. She eased into the bubbles and took her first full breath in hours.

"You sound better already." He smiled, relaxed as per his usual. "Come here."

She slipped through the water and he pulled her onto his lap.

"Do you feel better, too?" His arms cradling her, he kissed her temple.

"Much."

"Told you."

"Bragging is unattractive."

His laugh tumbled around in her chest, relaxing her further.

"Have you ever made love in a hot tub?" he rumbled into her ear.

"You've asked me this before." She turned and pressed a kiss to his mouth.

"Well, I must not have heard the answer I wanted if I'm asking again. So. Have you?"

"Is this another challenge to break one of my rules?"

"If so, will you say yes?" A wicked smile overtook his mouth. She couldn't resist.

She wrapped her arms around his neck and kissed him. His fingers speared into her hair, which she'd piled on top of her head in an effort to keep it dry.

The brisk wind chilled their shoulders, but they made their own heat. Her hands wandered down his chest to his lap and he cupped her breasts as he moved his mouth on the side of her neck.

What started out as touching graduated to more, and even though the last thing she should do was indulge in the man she couldn't keep, she couldn't help losing herself in him.

Back inside, she curled against him in bed, warm from the hot tub as well as their lovemaking. She relaxed against him, her arm thrown over his middle, her damp hair on his shoulder. She'd vowed to push everything Mags had said to her aside, but one thought looped in her mind like the lyrics of an overplayed song.

Mags had crowed about consequences, warning that they always found you. What had she meant by that? Maybe something, or maybe nothing. Hallie fell asleep without arriving at an answer. She woke in the morning, groggy, having dreamed most of the night.

She couldn't remember a single one of those dreams, but they'd left a film on her like a premonition of something bad to come.

Twenty

The following weekend, Hallie felt better about, well, everything. Presley was hosting another girls' night in. Cassandra and Hannah had arrived ahead of Hallie.

Hannah brought three pizzas. The pies were out, box tops open to allow the piping hot cheese to cool. "One cheese, one veggie, one with bacon and chicken," she announced.

They plated up and poured the wine. Hallie spilled a small amount into her glass. She'd been sipping cocktails practically nonstop since she'd started seeing Gavin. She'd forgotten how much eating and drinking happened while dating—a lot more than her usual.

Halfway through their second slices of pizza, Cassandra and Presley were discussing honeymoon destinations. Hannah had done nothing but delight them with tales of France, specifically about the romance of Paris. Hallie listened supportively, but as the only woman present who was not currently searching for a romantic getaway destination, it was hard not to feel left out.

"And the bread!" Hannah exclaimed. "Bread and cheese and wine is a religion over there. France is the perfect place for a honeymoon."

"It sounds like the perfect place to *live*." Cassandra smiled.

"I can't wait to visit Paris," Presley said on a sigh. "It's always been my dream to travel and write. I can't wait for Cash's world tour so I can sightsee."

"The only con is that wine makes me careless. I woke up several mornings missing my clothes," Hannah said.

"The case of the missing clothing," Presley said with a melodramatic gasp.

"I'm fairly certain the culprit was Will," Cassandra said with a giggle. Presley and Hannah howled with laughter. Hallie had to chuckle—her sister and Will were seriously cute together.

"Careful or else you'll end up pregnant before you know it," Pres warned. "And then who will help me drink wine?"

"Me!" Cassandra offered and the two women clinked glasses.

"I'm not sure *careful* matters when your period is as irregular as mine," Hannah said. "I could be pregnant now and wouldn't know it."

"You would know." Cassandra waved the idea off.

"Maybe not." Hannah shrugged one shoulder. "There

is a rumor that Banks ovaries thwart the effectiveness of birth control pills. How do you think Hallie and I were conceived?"

Hallie frowned at her sister. "Is that true?"

"According to Gram." Hannah shrugged. "So, even though I am on the pill, I'm never truly safe. Will is worth the risk."

"Well, sure. You're married now. If you *oops*-ed your way into a pregnancy everyone would be thrilled out of their minds." Cassandra made a follow-up joke about Hannah having twins, but Hallie was barely listening.

"I didn't know about the birth control thing," Hallie sort of repeated. She and Gavin had been *relying* on Hallie's birth control since the first time they'd slept together. And there had been a lot of times since.

"I'm sure it's an old wives' tale. Or Gram was trying to scare us into being careful when we did end up having sex," Hannah said.

"Hallie?" Presley, who picked up on everything unsaid, was watching Hallie closely. "What's going on with you? Does the wine taste okay?"

"This is our favorite vintage." Hannah frowned at her own glass.

"I think Pres is asking if the wine tastes okay *to Hallie*," Cassandra clarified. "Though, how would she know since she hasn't touched it."

Hallie's cheeks grew warm. Hannah's mouth fell open. "Oh my God. Tell me you were safe. You and Gavin. You were safe, right?"

"I was trying to break rules!" Hallie bleated. "I assumed my tried-and-true birth control worked until you trotted out a family horror story tonight." She'd had no reason to doubt her trusty pill until then.

"It's only been a few weeks since you two started seeing each other," Hannah said. "I'm sure you're fine."

"Well…" Presley started and every head in the room swiveled to her. "Cash and I had a scare a week ago and he bought about a dozen home tests in a panic. One of the tests claimed to be able to tell as soon as eight days after conception."

"Eight *days*?" Hallie asked, her voice hollow. She was going to be sick.

"Like Hannah said, you're probably fine," Presley said, her tone light. "But if you want to set your mind at ease, I have several tests leftover…"

"Oh God." Hallie shoved her plate aside. She couldn't think it.

"I'll take one, too," Hannah piped up. "Deal?"

"I don't know, Han…" Chances were, Hallie was fine. That her imagination had run wild on the heels of her conversation with Mags, the harbinger of doom.

"Come on, it will give us something to do," Cassandra chirped. "You can each take a test and then when they both read negative, we will switch from wine to shots of tequila."

More laughter rippled around the room, but Hallie didn't join in. Pregnancy would be a cruel outcome considering this was the one and only time in her life she'd broken so many of her own rules. Almost too cruel an outcome to imagine. Pregnant with a playboy's baby? That sounded like the title of a romance novel.

Hallie stood abruptly, drawing everyone's attention.

"Okay, now I have to take one, because I can't think of anything but my sister or me being pregnant."

"Super unlikely." Hannah stood, as well, giving Hallie a reassuring nod.

Cassandra, suffering no turmoil, clapped. "Let's do this!"

"I'll grab the tests." Pres returned a minute later with a pair of oblong, foil-wrapped pregnancy tests. "I brought one for each of you. They're very reliable. Three of my female coworkers back when I lived in Tallahassee swear by this brand. That's how I knew to tell Cash which brand to buy."

"As a journalist, you did your homework." Hallie gave her friend a wan smile as she accepted one of the tests for herself.

Pres pulled her into a quick hug and whispered, "You are going to be *fine*. Now go." She handed off the other test to Hannah. "You, too. Cassandra and I will be out here sipping wine and awaiting the results."

Hallie shut herself in the small half bathroom off the foyer while Hannah made her way to the main bathroom on the first floor. Thirty seconds later, Hallie had taken the test and set the pregnancy stick on the nearest flat surface—the edge of the sink. She took a few deep breaths while she waited for the results, which the package claimed took two minutes.

She might wait five, though. That's how much she didn't want to lay eyes on the results. She had a feeling, and it wasn't a good one, that Mags's warning had been more like an omen.

"Don't be silly," she addressed her reflection. "You're fine."

The chances of her getting pregnant were astronomical. She and Gavin hadn't used a condom, but they'd had sex only a few times. Well, okay, way more than a few times. Less than a dozen… Then Hallie did a quick count on her fingers and sent a worried look to her reflection again. Less than two dozen…

But.

She had been on birth control for *years*. She was regimented and routine about taking her pills. And even though her periods were random and untimely, surely there would be some other sign if she were pregnant.

A small voice in the back of her head whispered, *Even if you are only three weeks pregnant?*

Hallie couldn't listen to that voice right now. She had to listen to the voice of reason. And so, she thought of what Eleanor Banks might say. Would she tell her to keep her chin up? Would she advise her not to jump to conclusions? Would she be excited if Hallie was pregnant, or disappointed?

And how did Hallie feel? That was the most important question, wasn't it? Well, aside from how Gavin would feel. Oh, Lord, she couldn't think about that, either.

She opened her eyes when she heard chatter coming from the living room. Hannah's voice was the most prevalent, though Hallie couldn't hear what her sister was saying. Without looking at the results, she wrapped her hand around the pregnancy test and bolted from the bathroom. Hannah, wineglass in hand, clearly had her answer.

"Well?" Hallie asked anyway.

"Negative. I live to drink wine another day!" Hannah tapped her wineglass against Cassandra's. "What about you?"

"I'm too scared to look." Hallie held up the test. "Who wants to look for me?"

"I'll do it." Hannah relinquished her wineglass to the coffee table and walked over.

Hannah was Hallie's best friend. A person she would trust with her life. The person she could trust to read the pregnancy test and lay it out for her—whatever it read. Hallie handed over the test and watched Hannah's face as she read the results. When her sister's eyes tracked from the test back to Hallie, she didn't have to say a word for Hallie to know exactly what the test said.

"Oh, shit," Presley murmured, picking up on the silence between them.

"It could be wrong," Hannah said. "You can go to a doctor and double-check."

"Oh my God," Cassandra muttered.

Hallie snatched the test. Two bold pink lines might as well have been a pair of middle fingers flipping off her future plans. "It's not wrong."

Somehow she knew. Not only because the red wine wasn't appetizing, or because Mags's warning of "consequences" was timely, but because if Fate was real and Karma was the bitch everyone said she was, then *of course* Hallie would be pregnant.

Maybe her gut had been warning her away from Gavin all along. All those years of avoiding talking to him or approaching him.

He'd made her feel bulletproof, and she'd forgotten the reasons to be careful. She'd ignored that speeding, even on a back country road, could lead to an accident. She'd ignored that diving into ice-cold water could cause hypothermia. And she'd certainly ignored that birth control pills were not 100 percent effective. Especially, apparently, in her and her sister's cases.

"I'm an idiot," she said, her voice thin.

"No. You're not." Hannah touched Hallie's shoulder.

"Yeah. I am." A rogue wave of dizziness crested and Hallie reached for the sofa. When she lowered onto a cushion, she was immediately surrounded by her sister and her friends. She should've been grateful, but she was going through the blame phase of grief.

"This is your fault." She pointed at Presley. "You were the one encouraging me to approach Gavin. I'm not ready to have a baby." She had been trying to break out of her shell and learn more about herself, not create another human being she'd be responsible for over the next eighteen years.

And Gavin—what the hell was she supposed to tell *him*? He had no interest in settling down. Which was fine when they were *just* dating and *just* having sex. A baby would drastically change those temporary plans.

"Life is beautiful and happens in the order it should," Presley consoled her. "Cash and I stumbled our way to happily-ever-after, you know. We didn't plan to have a years-long break in between falling in love with each other again."

"Gavin is not Cash," Hallie reminded Presley.

Presley gave her a tight-lipped smile. If Hallie was

expecting reassurance, it didn't come. Cash and Presley had been college sweethearts. Cash had loved her even when he'd broken up with her and left Florida. Presley had fallen back in love with him when she returned to Beaumont Bay—if she'd ever fallen out.

There were few similarities to Hallie and Gavin's story. She'd made a deal with the devilishly sexy Sutherland brother, agreeing to follow him wherever he led, no strings attached. And now she was pregnant with his baby.

"There are options," Cassandra reminded her gently. "Do what's right for you."

Hannah exchanged glances with Hallie. Hannah knew Hallie's heart. And so did Hallie. As much of a surprise as this pregnancy was, there was no way she wouldn't welcome a baby into her world.

"Is anyone else tired of wine?" Cassandra asked, clearly in support. "I saw Sprite in your fridge, didn't I, Pres?"

"Great idea." Presley stood. "Hallie? Hannah?"

"We'll drink Sprite. Won't we?" Hannah rubbed her sister's back.

Hallie nodded. Her friends bustled around refilling plates with extra slices of pizza and pouring clear soda into tumblers before garnishing them with wedges of lime. They weren't willing to let Hallie dwell on the life-altering news she'd just learned. But there was something she'd have to do, and soon.

"I have to tell Gavin," Hallie announced as she accepted a glass of soda from Cassandra. About the pregnancy, as well as another reality she didn't want to think about. Her and Gavin's affair had reached its end. They couldn't continue having fun with a baby on the way. A baby was serious. And "serious" wasn't what he was looking for. He'd said so himself.

"You can tell him when you're ready." Hannah held up her glass. "I promise I won't say anything to anyone until you do. I won't even tell Will."

"What Cash doesn't know won't hurt him," Presley agreed as she held up her glass.

"And Luke is fine in the dark. I think he prefers it." Cassandra's glass joined the other two as they all looked to Hallie expectantly.

Hallie tapped her glass with the others. "Thanks. All of you. I appreciate your support."

"Whatever you choose to do," Pres said, "about the pregnancy or Gavin, we have your back."

Cassandra and Hannah agreed, and then they all drank on it.

Twenty-One

Gavin missed not seeing Hallie last night. He'd considered deterring her from going out, but he was not the clingy sort. He didn't used to be, anyway. At least he hadn't had to sit at home alone.

Since Cash had been booted out of his house that night, too, he'd called Will and Luke and Gavin. The four of them had met at the studio to talk shop and down a few cold beers. Luckily for Gav, his brothers had mostly talked about work and sports rather than busting his balls over Hallie. Ironically, they would have been right to. He'd been out with the boys, having a good time, and yet she'd consumed most of his thoughts.

He'd arrived home to empty sheets. Going to bed alone hadn't been a big deal for him before he'd met

Hallie, but he'd had trouble sleeping without her. So.
That had been mildly alarming.

This morning he'd woken, made coffee and rubbed
the achy, empty feeling in the center of his chest. He'd
blamed it on heartburn at first but after he'd texted her
and invited her over, the mysterious ache vanished. She'd
put him off until afternoon, but he didn't care when she
came as long as she did. He couldn't wait to hold her
close, to kiss her plush mouth, to strip her naked and
be inside her.

He shoved his needy feelings aside and prepared
lunch, slapping a couple of turkey sandwiches together
with pickles, lettuce, mayonnaise and mustard. By the
time he was opening a fresh bag of potato chips, a
knock came.

His girl was here.

He raced to open the front door. "It's not locked.
Why are you knocking?"

Hallie's smile was pained, her shoulders stiff. Fear
skittered up his spine. He dismissed it. He'd read too
much into how he'd been feeling about her already and
refused to indulge in further idiocy.

"Come on in and take off all your clothes," he invited
with a grin. "Then you can knock me over with one of
those kisses of yours."

Hallie bit her lip, her throat moving as she swallowed.

Not good, his mind warned.

Shut up, he told it plainly.

He was familiar with this version of Hallie. The serious version who had a hard time talking to him—who could scarcely *look* at him.

"What's wrong?" he couldn't help asking. If she laid it out for him, then he could work with what he knew.

"The reason I came here today," she started, her tone formal. His stomach sank. He'd had a bad feeling all damn morning and with an opener like that, how could it possibly get better?

"Will you come in first? It's freezing out there."

She indulged him and stepped inside, but she didn't remove her coat. Another sign something was terribly wrong.

"It's time we wrap things up," she stated, her tone robotic. "We avoided being entangled over Thanksgiving, but Christmas is a harder holiday to dodge."

He blinked. What was she talking about?

"We knew this was temporary, so there's no sense in drawing more attention and speculation from everyone." Her mouth flinched into a smile that didn't reach her eyes. "I had fun, though."

"Hals—"

She offered her hand. He glared at her outstretched palm and then at her placid face. "Are you offering to shake my hand right now?"

"That's how this started. Wouldn't it make sense we end it the same way?"

"Why are we ending at all? Did something happen last night?" He didn't think Hannah, Cassandra and Presley were against him, but he could be wrong. They would have had to have said something for Hallie to have done a one-eighty.

"Gavin." She lowered her arm. "I can be professional about this if you can. And I know you can since you are incredibly professional. We've had our fun, but we're going to have to see each other in the workplace again. We have shared clients. I would like to keep sharing clients. I like you."

Why did her proclamation hurt so much? He liked her, too—a whole hell of a lot—way too much to let her dump him in his foyer.

"You like me," he repeated numbly, "but you don't want to have sex with me anymore."

His mind raced. What had he done wrong? He knew she'd been off-kilter at Mags Dumond's party, but they'd ironed everything out after. Hallie had spent the night in his arms.

"If Mags got into your head—" he started.

"It's not that," she interrupted.

How could she show up at his house and so casually break up with him? Had what they'd done together meant nothing to her? He'd missed her last night terribly, and while he'd lain in bed alone wishing she was next to him, she'd been…what? Plotting how to let him down easy? Planning on telling him she never wanted to sleep with him again?

"I'm going to try to explain this with as few swear words as possible." Anger was the wrong emotion for this situation, but he couldn't help himself. At least his warning elicited a reaction from her. Her hazel eyes grew wide and wary. "I'm not remotely done with you. I'm not letting you walk away like there's nothing happening between us." He'd been questioning everything he thought he knew about relationships since he and Hallie started hanging out. He'd obliterated his own boundary lines in the process of helping her walk over her own. He wouldn't let her go easily, if ever.

"We have to stop sometime."

Her glib response pissed him off more, which made him say exactly the wrong thing. "I upended my life for you."

"Well, I'm so sorry for the inconvenience," she said with a mirthless laugh.

"That came out wrong." He put his hand to his forehead, trying to sort his thoughts and explain. "What I meant to say was that I stopped dating for you." Shit. That sounded worse.

Her mouth dropped open, confirming he was digging a deeper hole the more he talked. "Good news, Gav. You are now free to date as many people as you'd like." She turned for the door.

"Hallie, wait. That didn't come out right, either." God, why was it so hard to tell her what he knew? That she belonged with him—in his bed, in his life. That whatever had scared her off was something they could tackle together. "What I meant to say was—" he swallowed thickly, struggling to find the words "—you weren't the only one breaking rules."

She faced him, her gaze softening.

"We're having fun," he said, hoping like hell she'd agree. "Right?"

"We *had* fun." Her voice was hollow. "But fun has a way of turning serious. How serious do you want to be with me?"

He took a literal step away from her, a fresh wave of fear oozing through him. "What do you mean?"

She gestured at the space between them. "Your single status is in grave danger if we keep doing what we're doing."

Ice slipped into his belly. In his mind, relationships had always been the enemy of freedom. Right now he could do what he wanted, when he wanted. And, he thought until two minutes ago that Hallie was on the same page as him. Willing to be in his bed and on his arm, but with no real commitment making them prisoners to each other.

Then he thought about where she'd spent the evening last night—with three very happily engaged or married women. It wasn't hard to figure out what had happened. Hannah cooing over her trip to Paris. Presley and Cassandra chattering about wedding plans.

"You want more," he said.

She pulled her shoulders back. Looked him in the eyes. When she spoke, her voice was calm and cool. "And you don't."

There was no elegant way to admit to that, so instead he said, "I like what we have, Hals. I thought we agreed not to label it."

"I was wrong." Her smile was sad instead of upset this time. "I want to go back to being friends with you. Or, well, start being friends with you. I don't think I could bear it if we argued every time we saw each other. We are friends, right?"

"Of course," he agreed as a sinking feeling hollowed out his gut. *Friends* wasn't enough for him. "I take it this means you aren't coming to my family's house on Christmas Eve."

"It would make things harder." Warmth leaked into her gaze, briefly reminding him of every sensual hour he'd spent with her. He was going to miss that look. "We need space to make the transition work. Just for a while. I'm sure we'll be back to normal soon enough."

Before she walked out of his house, and apparently out of his *life*, he reached for her hand. "Hals."

She turned.

"Are you sure?" He waited, his heart thrashing in his chest. Hope bubbled up inside him when she smiled but it died a quick death when she nodded her head. There wasn't hope in her eyes, but resolution.

He glided his thumb over her hand, missing her already. "I want more than friendship with you, but if that's my only option…"

He hazarded a glance at her, hoping she'd change her mind, run into his arms and tell him she was wrong. Instead, she said, "Thank you, Gavin."

"Sure," he said around a lump in his throat. Then she pulled her hand from his and left. He watched her car back out of his driveway, wanting more than anything to chase her, beg her if he had to, but he only stood and watched her go.

She wanted more. And *more* was the one thing not in his plans. *More* scared the crap out of him. There was no proof in his past suggesting he'd make a good boyfriend, let alone a good husband. He couldn't ask Hallie to risk her own future when he might well fail at what his three brothers had been handling with alarming grace.

He took a look around at the high ceilings and expansive kitchen. His gargantuan new house mocked him. He'd built a veritable mansion with multiple rooms for himself. Hallie had just reminded him he was going to remain in it alone for a good long while.

He rubbed his chest again, the ache intensifying. This was ridiculous. He cared about her enough to let her take what she needed from him. She'd stepped into her own, like he'd wanted.

And, hell, what was he upset about? He'd had the best damn time of his life. He'd known going in that they would eventually move on. And it wasn't like she hated him. She'd said herself she wanted to remain friends, that she wanted to work with him professionally. That, too, should've been enough.

So why isn't it?

The ache in his chest wasn't heartburn. It was regret. A whole truckload of it.

Hallie might still be in his life, but nothing would be the same. He could see her but not touch her. He could smile at her, but not flirt with her. And he would continue climbing into bed, beneath a giant painting of an ice cream sundae she'd chosen for him, without her by his side.

That sucked.

"Oh, honey! I'm so excited!" Eleanor Banks clapped her hands together. "We have to celebrate. I'm glad I baked a pie."

It was a few days before Christmas Eve and Eleanor was wearing a gaudy reindeer sweater she'd knitted
herself. As were Hallie and Hannah. "Tradition" in the
Banks house was more a requirement.

Gram returned from the kitchen with three plates
of chocolate pie balanced in both hands. She set two of
the plates on the wide coffee table and lifted her own.
She speared her pie with a fork, pausing before she ate
a bite. "I wish your parents could be here to hear the
news in person. But you know how they hate traveling
during the holidays."

Hallie wished the same. Her parents weren't neces-
sarily uninvolved in her life, but they didn't do things
the way everyone else's parents did. She didn't resent
them for it, but she did miss them. Now, in particular.

Hallie had been thinking a lot lately about what kind
of parent she would be. What traditions to start for her
own family. Which made her think of Gavin, and sent
a dagger straight through her heart.

When she'd arrived at his house, she'd fully intended
on telling him she was pregnant. By the time they were
having that horrible conversation, she hadn't had the
courage. When she'd practiced the breakup speech in
the mirror, she thought she knew what to expect. She
thought he'd smile, offer a "Come on, Hals, you don't
have to do this," and then hug her and acquiesce.

That hadn't been what had happened. She'd felt her
own heart breaking when he'd been upset, when he'd
gently taken her hand. When he'd argued passionately
instead of casually.

Meanwhile, her heart had been crumbling. It'd taken

every bit of her willpower not to burst into tears and rush into his arms. He'd have let her come back. He'd have taken her to bed and held her, and he would have told her everything was going to be okay. But she knew something he didn't. She was pregnant with his child, and he was not going to be "okay" with that.

So. She'd chickened out. Once he'd agreed he didn't want more, what else had there been to say? They'd originally agreed to keep things easy. A baby was about a million levels up from easy.

"You're going to be an amazing mom," Hannah said as she speared her own pie with a fork.

"Well, of course she is." Gram's hot-pink lips parted into a sweet smile. "She was raised by me. I'm a great mom."

"The best." Hallie squeezed her Gram's hand. Eleanor Banks had raised twin granddaughters, given them her name and balanced a life of fame and fortune. It was admirable. "You are the perfect example."

"Don't be too hard on your own mama." Gram waved pink fingernails matching her lipstick. "My daughter was always a bit of the gypsy. She was born that way. There's nothing wrong with dancing to your own tune. And she gave me a chance to raise you girls. What a blessing."

"We feel the same way," Hannah said, echoing Hallie's thoughts.

"Hallie, you will be the kind of mom you were meant to be. Why, your child is going to be smothered with love given how close the Sutherlands are." Gram lifted her manicured eyebrows. "How is Gavin taking the news?"

Hallie had purposely left out that she hadn't told Gavin. Hannah knew, of course. She'd hounded Hallie until she'd admitted she hadn't had the courage to tell him.

"He'll be a wonderful father," Gram said supportively, reaching for Hallie's hand.

Hallie agreed wholeheartedly. But when she opened her mouth to speak, she burst into tears. When she was able to pull herself together, she recited a garbled version of what happened at Gavin's house three days ago. How she'd shown up to tell him. How, even though he was visibly shaken, he hadn't offered her the more she so desperately needed.

"I couldn't tell him about the baby. I was afraid…" Hallie's voice cut off and she realized there wasn't any more to say. *Afraid* summed up everything.

Eleanor looked to Hannah, who translated while stroking Hallie's back. "She broke up with him because she thought it was better to do it sooner than later. Especially with the holidays around the corner. He told her he was not the settling down kind, so she figured it would be best to handle the pregnancy by herself." Hannah wrapped an arm around Hallie's shoulders. "I reminded her she was far from alone."

"That's right, sweetheart. Hannah and I are here for you." Gram patted Hallie's leg. "Don't cry on your pie. Life throws you all sorts of curveballs, but you are a Banks. You can handle this with one eye shut, one hand tied behind your back *and* while hopping on one leg."

Hallie laughed through her tears, her grandmother's

silly visual helping to lighten her mood. Hallie wasn't alone—she'd never been alone. "Thank you, Gram."

"You're welcome, sweetheart. Do you want Hannah and me to sing to you?"

"Always." A duet from her sister and her grandmother would make her feel better. She would tell Gavin the truth—that they had made a baby—soon enough. She'd gone to the doctor yesterday to make *triple* sure she was pregnant, even after taking a second home pregnancy test the morning she'd shown up at Gavin's house. Every test had been positive.

The doctor was happy with Hallie's blood work and general health. She'd sent Hallie out the door with prenatal vitamins and a big smile, assuring Hallie they'd see a lot more of each other over the next nine months or so.

An unexpected wave of joy had crashed into her then. She hadn't planned on being pregnant, but already loved the bean incubating in her womb. Her grandmother and her sister were overjoyed, which made it easier for Hallie to picture a bright future for her daughter or son.

Yet a shadow loomed. She'd never planned on being pregnant while nursing a broken heart.

She knew better than anyone that every family looked different. Her parents hadn't raised her, but were still in her life. She had her grandmother and her sister. Gavin would be a part of his child's life, she knew. He might panic or freak out when he learned the news—to be fair, so had she—but he'd step up and be the father he was capable of being.

They would develop their own routine, arrange visits with their child, attend parent-teacher conferences together at school. It would work out.

Hallie and Hannah hadn't had a typical childhood—how could they when they were raised by one of country music's biggest stars?—but they'd never lacked love. Just because Gavin wasn't interested in settling down, didn't mean he wouldn't love their child. And his family—the Sutherlands—would love their child, as well.

Hannah would be an aunt and Will would be an uncle. Eleanor would be a great-grandmother. Presley and Cassandra would soon be married to the two other Sutherland brothers, making them "official" aunts. Her child would be loved by many and that's what mattered.

Or so she tried to convince her fractured heart whenever it argued with her. Hallie had done the unthinkable. She'd fallen in love with Gavin. She had been in love with him for some time—possibly since she'd first laid eyes on him.

As her sister and her grandmother sang about never giving up, Hallie felt herself smile. There was much to celebrate. A baby was an exciting event. She'd keep doing the next best thing for her child and everything would work out.

Hallie was a family girl and that's what she and Gavin had unwittingly started. A family. Her heart gave a mournful wail, and she wondered how long it would take for her to fall out of love with Gavin.

Or if she could.

Twenty-Two

Christmas Eve would've been happier with Hallie at his side.

At his parents' house, dinner had been fine but the conversation had felt forced. As if the couples ringing the table—every one of his brothers would happen to be in happy relationships right now, wouldn't they?—had been trying too hard not to mention The Breakup.

Or so he'd thought.

The presents had been opened and his father was taking a bag of discarded wrapping paper to the curb while his mom swept into the bar area holding a tray of mugs filled with hot cocoa. She mentioned "homemade marshmallows" and Luke volleyed by suggesting spiking the cocoa with Bailey's Irish Cream. Gavin opened his mouth to say "make mine a double" but before he could, a hand wrapped around his arm.

"Oh, no you don't." Presley's fire-red hair matched her mood. "Come with us."

He glanced over his shoulder to find Hannah and Cassandra standing sentinel, their unhappy expressions mirroring Presley's.

"What's going on?"

Pres responded by tugging on his arm. He let her drag him from the bar and into the adjoining room where they'd opened gifts. Boxes holding clothes, bath soaps, trinkets and other gifts were stacked next to everyone's respective seats.

"What's wrong? None of you liked the gifts I bought you?" He'd been trying for levity but was met with answering glares.

"This isn't about gifts," Hannah stated.

Hell, he knew that. "What did you three say to Hallie, anyway?"

The girls exchanged looks.

"She spent one evening in your company and then came to my house and dumped me on my ass."

Hannah turned to Cassandra. "I'm not sure whether to verbally berate him or physically castrate him." Gavin looked toward the bar. His brothers were happily pouring spirits into their cocoa and ignoring him completely. He was on his own.

"Verbally would be cleaner," Cassandra said, her voice uncharacteristically cold.

"I'll start." Presley faced Gavin. "You are a moron for letting Hallie go. You are a self-centered, bullheaded pig with your head up your ass. Do you think you can actually do any better than *Hallie Banks*?"

"I second all of that," Hannah said. "Wholeheartedly."

"Especially the part about his head in his ass," Cassandra agreed.

"Don't blame me," he argued. "I had fun with Hallie." He kept his voice down so the rest of his family couldn't hear. Another lecture from his brothers was the last thing he needed. "And I'm not only talking about sex."

"So, you have your first argument and you let her *leave*?" Cassandra frowned.

"She was clear about what she wanted."

"So were you. You want to be unattached. She was too much for you to deal with." Hannah squared her jaw.

"Now hang on—" He held up a hand in his defense.

Presley pointed at the sofa. "Sit."

"No, I don't think I will." He wasn't positive they wouldn't hog-tie him and do a host of other unpleasant things he'd rather not consider.

"We've kept quiet long enough." This from Hannah. Presley and Cassandra shot the blonde wide-eyed warnings. Hannah rolled her eyes. "I don't mean about *that*."

"What do you all know?" he asked, his head swiveling to take in the three women content to bust his balls.

"Don't change the subject," Hannah snapped. "Do you want Hallie in your life or not?"

"As more than a friend?" Cassandra tacked on.

"Have you admitted to yourself what you're feeling?" Presley poked him in the chest with her pointy fingers. "Spoiler alert. That's not heartburn."

He rubbed the center of his chest, uncomfortable for myriad reasons. He'd prefer not to have this discussion firing-squad style. He didn't want to have it on Christmas Eve, either. And he sure as hell didn't want to admit what he'd since figured out in the long, lonely days that had passed since Hallie dumped him. It was devastating to realize he was in love with a woman who didn't want him.

He sagged on the couch. "I want her. You don't think I know she's worth fighting for? I'm in love with her and terrified she's going to turn me down. Do you know how hard that is for me to admit? Especially when you three hate me as much as she does."

Presley's hand landed on top of his. She didn't squeeze the life out of his fingers but instead offered a comforting pat. "We don't hate you. More importantly, Hallie doesn't hate you. I promise that's not why she broke up with you."

"Then why won't she return my calls or my texts? Why *did* she break up with me? If I've learned one thing it's when a woman is ready to leave, they leave."

"And your policy is to let them?" Cassandra asked.

He'd always had trouble with that part. He preferred to do the breaking up whenever possible. The fear of failing miserably had kept his past relationships short and shallow. And now that he was in love, possibly for the first time, the stakes couldn't be any higher.

"By then there's usually nothing left to fight for," he murmured.

So not the case with Hallie. He had agonized over losing her for too many sleepless nights and too many tumultuous days. The man he knew himself to be had been wrestling with the man emerging now. He loved her, but she'd made her decision. He had no idea if he could change her mind.

"I don't know what she wants," he admitted, and hating how it sounded like defeat. "I'm afraid what I offer won't be enough." After all, what they'd had hadn't been enough for her.

Hannah sighed. Cassandra echoed that sigh with one of her own. Their gazes were soft, almost sad. When he thought he'd won over his sister-in-law and two future sisters-in-law, Presley turned on him.

"Do *not* give up. Especially if what you said is true. You love her? Man up and tell her."

"Pres, she asked for space."

"Women don't know what they want," Cassandra said. "If you loved her, you would go to her right this second and confess that you're a miserable bastard and can't bear the idea of living without her. Are you waiting for a guarantee she'll take you back? Spoiler alert, there are no guarantees."

"How can you stand living another day without her?" Hannah asked. "Isn't it obvious she was missing today?"

Yes. It was. The chair at the dinner table sat empty next to him, a literal reminder of what he'd lost. His family had arranged themselves around the barren chair as if holding vigil for the woman who should have absolutely been by his side.

"I know what you're trying to do," he said, "and I know you love Hallie as much as I do…"

Three sets of eyebrows slammed over three adorable noses.

He licked his lips and gave in. They were right. He'd let fear and the uncertainty of the future make his decisions for him. He'd never been more disappointed in himself. "I'll talk to her, okay?"

"That's all we ask," Presley said sweetly. "Who wants hot cocoa?"

"I do," Hannah and Cassandra said as they stood.

"Don't breathe a word about this to your brothers," Presley threatened Gavin.

"And don't tell Hallie," Hannah added.

"Go get 'em, tiger." Cassandra elbowed him on her way out.

The girls dispersed, leaving him alone. He stayed on the sofa for a moment, hands folded in front of him as he thought through what had just happened.

A confession he hadn't planned on making, especially to the women who would totally use it against him the first chance they got. But he couldn't regret saying it. He *was* in love with Hallie. Which explained why he'd been feeling like garbage.

Was Cassandra right? Was it possible Hallie didn't know what she wanted? Had she made a preemptive strike, ending things before he could to save herself from heartbreak? And, the biggest question of all: If he confessed he was ready for the *more* she'd spoken about, was it too late to win her back?

Hallie was the only person who could answer those questions. He needed to talk to her, and he needed to do it right away. When he stepped from the room, every member of his family and extended family paused, cocoa mugs in hand, and watched him expectantly.

"Where is she?" he asked Hannah. "At home?"

Hannah nodded and gave him her first genuine smile of the evening.

"Do not call her and tell her I'm coming," he said, including Cassandra and Presley in his request.

"I won't," Hannah promised. Presley and Cassandra each swore their allegiance to silence.

"What's going on?" Will asked.

"Hopefully he's going to tell Hallie he's been a major ass," Cash offered.

"Apologizing on your knees is incredibly emasculating, but worth it in the end." Luke grinned, as if he liked the vision of his youngest brother begging for forgiveness.

"I'll do what I have to do," Gavin said, and he meant it.

Hallie was grateful the health food store was open on Christmas Eve. She wanted to stock up on vitamins and healthy juices. For whatever reason she'd had an almost debilitating craving for sweet potato chips, so she'd picked up a bag of those, as well.

She pulled into her driveway, smiling at the small Christmas tree glowing in the window of her apartment. Last night she'd thought it looked lonely there, but she woke in higher spirits today. Reusable tote slung over her shoulder, she stepped from her car and into the crisp winter air.

She refused to feel sorry for spending Christmas Eve

alone. Gram had invited her to a party and Hallie had been the one to say no. She wasn't in a partying mood.

Hannah had gone to the Sutherland house for dinner and had tried to convince Hallie to come with her. Hallie politely refused. She was too fragile, the breakup with Gavin far too fresh. The last thing the Sutherlands needed was a Banks sister crying on their holiday ham.

Besides, she and Hannah would go to Gram's for Christmas breakfast tomorrow morning to exchange gifts and sing carols. Will would be there, of course. Wherever Hannah was from now until the end of time, Will would be there, too. Just seeing him would remind Hallie of Gavin, or maybe Will would bring him up. That was something she'd have to get used to, as well.

And who knew, it might work out for the best if Hallie and Gavin grew accustomed to not being together before she broke the news about the pregnancy. She didn't want him to agree to be with her under duress. She wanted him to love her. As much as she loved him.

He'd sent several texts over the last few days, each some version of "can we talk?"

She'd admit, they did need to talk. And they would. As soon as she decided the best way to tell him he was going to be a father. The delay wasn't only for him. The longer she waited, the more time she'd have to bandage her broken heart when he ultimately told her he couldn't stay with her and raise their child. She almost hated how much she wished he'd say the opposite.

As much as she'd favored her independence in the past, though, now it made her incredibly sad. She was in love with Gavin, and she didn't want to fall out of love with him. She was carrying his child, for goodness' sake. Of course she loved him.

The pregnancy had been a shock, but the prospect of having a child—of having *his* child—excited her. Their baby would be beautiful if it shared even a single strand of his DNA. And maybe she and Gavin would be great at raising a child together but separately. She and Hannah had been raised in an unorthodox manner, and they'd had a wonderful childhood.

Last night, their mother had called Hallie to say Merry Christmas. Their conversation was warm and loving. She told her mother she had news to share but preferred to share it in person. Her mother hadn't pressed for Hallie to tell her right away. She'd said she respected Hallie's choices and they could do a video call tomorrow night if she was available. Hallie had felt better instantly.

Her heart would mend on its own time. She was strong and could do anything she set her mind to. Ironically, it was Gavin who had helped her understand that.

Tonight, she'd spend Christmas Eve alone watching a holiday movie with her arm elbow-deep in a bag of sweet potato chips. There were worse ways to spend an evening. Just when she'd convinced herself, a truck pulled in behind her and blew her plans to smithereens.

She stood in the doorway of her apartment as Gavin stepped out of his gray F-150. He looked good, dressed in dark blue jeans and a button-down shirt open at the collar, hat perched on his head. The leather jacket was doing wonders for him in the "bad boy" department. It wasn't hard to see why she'd asked him to help her break rules. It was as if God had crafted him to be a rebel.

But that had been an excuse, she admitted to herself as he approached her in a few long-legged steps. She had wanted an excuse to be close to him. It'd been all she'd wanted for as long as she could remember. And now that he was walking toward her, her porch light illuminating his handsome face, all she wanted was to be close to him again.

The question was, should she let herself?

Twenty-Three

Gavin tried to read Hallie's mind as he approached but came up empty. She could be preparing another lecture. He worried it might be a loud one ending with her telling him to go home, but maybe—just maybe—she'd invite him in.

If he made it inside, would she let him down again, this time wishing him a lovely Christmas by himself, or would she hear him out, and reconsider her decision to leave?

There was only one way to find out.

"Hey," he said, which was not the best opener. He hadn't exactly crafted a plan. He'd driven here like a bat out of hell, straight from his parents' house, when he should've taken a long, slow drive on a dark country road while he thought about the best way to approach her. Instead, here he was, with a half-baked plan that involved nothing less than wearing his still-beating heart on his sleeve.

He prayed that was enough.

She looked beautiful—and more vulnerable than he'd ever seen her. She wore jeans and a soft pink sweater, cowboy boots and, like him, a leather jacket.

"I like your coat." He offered a nervous smile. "Does this mean I've made a rule-breaker out of you after all?"

"You have no idea," she replied with a cautious smile. Cautious or no, he'd take it.

"May I carry that for you?" He reached for the tote resting on her shoulder.

She handed it over, giving him an excuse to follow her inside. Not quite an invitation, but again, he'd take it.

In the kitchen, she made short work of unpacking the groceries. She left out a bag of chips.

"I'd ask you to stay for dinner, but I assume you already ate." She lifted the chips. "This is my dinner. Far from gourmet."

"I didn't come here for dinner," he confessed. Hannah was right. Presley was right. Cassandra was right. He'd had his head in his ass. It was easier to see all the things he loved about Hallie when she was standing in front of him. It was also impossible to accept her friendship alone when he knew they were capable of so much more.

"I screwed up the other night," he said, pulling his hat off his head and resting it on the kitchen table. *Here went nothing.* "I let you believe you were a pastime instead of telling you what you mean to me. To be fair, I thought it was heartburn and not heartbreak." He put his hand on his chest and her eyes followed the movement. His heart thumped hard against his palm, kicking his rib cage when it should have been kicking his ass. How could he have been so clueless?

"Speeding on a back road, skinny-dipping in the ice-cold lake, PDA on the boardwalk. Those things, I did for you. But not *only* for you. I benefited, too—probably more than you did. *Definitely* more than you did," he corrected, clearing his throat. This wasn't easy, but he wasn't giving up. Not this time. "You might not know this, Hals, but while I was helping you break your rules, you were busting my heart out of the prison cell I was keeping it in. I have never allowed myself to feel deeply for a woman before. I was convinced loving someone meant missing out on life. You taught me being in love made life better. How could I possibly miss out on life when you're the one who makes my life worth living?"

She continued staring at him, her expression giving away nothing. He took a deep breath and willed himself to keep going.

"You made me a better person in the weeks we spent together. You made me fall in love with you, too. And trust me, Hals, I have no clue what I'm doing when it comes to being in love. I'm the biggest risk you could take. I love you. I love you, and if you still want to dump me, you better have a damn good reason. Because I'm not giving up on us anytime soon. You might've sent me for a spin a few days ago, but I've recalibrated. I know what I want. *You*."

Her eyebrows bent in sympathy.

"I'm about to break the biggest rule in my world and

beg you for forever." His hands shook, but not because he was scared or nervous. They shook because he knew she was his future. He was willing to fight for her. He was willing to beg—on his knees.

He lowered onto her floor and took one of her hands in his. "Will you take me back? Will you come back to my bed, back to my house, back into my life? I vow to be the best boyfriend you've ever had. And eventually, if you want, more than that. One day I'll be down here with a diamond ring in my hand, and you'll say yes because you're so in love with me there'll be no other answer. You won't be able to believe the man I've become—the man your love changed me into."

She was frozen, staring down at him, her mouth open softly. He was starting to sweat. He wasn't sure what her reaction would be, but he thought he'd at least see a smile. He'd *hoped* she'd sling her arms around his neck and kiss him senseless.

Instead she put her hand to her forehead like she was checking for a fever. "Remember what you said about having a family? About having children?"

"Uh…" Well, damn, that threw him. He kept hold of her hand, his other hand on the kitchen counter as he stood. Her eyes tracked his movements, her chin tilting up. He didn't dare let her go. Now that he was touching her, he didn't want to stop.

"The night you asked if twins ran in my family, and I asked you if you wanted a big family," she reminded him.

"Right. Yeah." He remembered. He'd said something

about being a bachelor, about how settling down wasn't for him. "Not my finest moment."

"What changed?"

He didn't have to think about his answer. "You. You changed everything. You changed *me*. It might have taken me a minute to absorb what was all around me, but Hallie. Honey." He smiled down at her. "I'd settle down with you. It wouldn't even be settling. I'd have a family with you, no question. You and I would make beautiful babies."

Her eyelashes fluttered. He'd surprised her, which seemed only fair since he'd surprised himself. He imagined their future child and a grin took over his face. A baby girl with her golden eyes, or a baby boy with his wavy hair…maybe one of each. Yeah. Hell, yeah.

She cocked her head to the side, her gentle vulnerability shining through. "Do you mean it?"

He cupped her sweet face in his palms. "Yes. I'd have everything with you. I would have *anything* with you. I'm considering things I never considered before I was with you. My brain was in the way. *Fear* was in the way. Now I know better. I had a trial run without you and I nearly had a heart attack. I don't want to miss you anymore. If that means upending my entire world to give you what you want—what *we* want—that's an easy ask. Just…reconsider, okay? I don't want to do this without you."

That must've been the right thing to say, because she threw herself at him. He caught her, staggering backward a step before regaining his footing and holding her tightly in his arms. She felt right there. Like she belonged there. His heart thundered against his chest as if it was reaching for hers. She tipped her chin to kiss him and he didn't hesitate kissing her back. When they parted, the most beautiful words came out of her mouth.

"I love you, too."

Happiness unfurled in his chest. Before he could revel in the feeling of being loved by Hallie Banks, she rocked him with three more words he hadn't seen coming.

"And I'm pregnant."

His turn to be shocked down to his boots. "I—what?"

"You didn't know, did you?"

He shook his head. Or thought he did. He couldn't feel anything from the neck up.

"I'm only three and a half weeks along," she said, still holding on to him, and thank God or else he might've fallen on his ass. "I'm terrified now that you know, you'll take back every beautiful thing you said. I didn't mean for this to happen, but I'm really, really happy about it. I didn't want to pressure you into a future you hadn't planned on, so I hadn't decided how to tell you."

"Pregnant," he repeated, trying to wrap his head around the news. "You're serious."

"I'm serious. And you should know, before you say anything else, there is a very good chance I'm pregnant with twins."

"Twins?" Now he did feel like he might fall over. But it wasn't because he was upset. No, definitely not upset. He didn't have to dig deep to find the love he felt for Hallie easily extended to the unborn child—or children—in her belly. His love for her instantly grew bigger and bolder than before, and he hadn't known that was possible.

A smile crawled across his face, and, almost cautiously, she returned it with one of her own.

"Are you telling me there's a baby on the way, and it's mine? That I'm going to be a dad and you're going to be a mom, and if we're really lucky, we could end up being parents to not one but *two* babies?"

Her eyes shined as she grinned up at him. "Yes, I am."

He kissed her again, his tongue sparring with hers. She clutched him tight, her fingers winding in the strands of his hair.

When he pulled away, he took one look at the dimples denting her cheeks and said, "Rule breaking suits us, gorgeous. And just so you understand where my head's at," he said, "I meant everything I said before you shared your news with me. I want you in my life. I want you in my house. I want you in my hot tub, in my car, making out with me on the boardwalk…"

"I get the point." Her laugh was musical and happy.

"Can you forgive me for letting you walk out of my life?"

She nodded, fresh tears welling in her eyes.

"It'll never happen again, Hals. No matter what, I will fight for you." He swiped her tears away with the pads of his thumbs. "And our family."

Their next kiss grew deeper. She pulled at his clothes. He tore at hers. They didn't make it to the bedroom, instead making love on the couch, right beside her tabletop Christmas tree.

Epilogue

"Gavin and Hallie really do have the best view," Presley conceded as she sat in the lawn chair next to her husband's. Cash grunted his disagreement.

"Why, thank you," Hallie answered. She was stretched out, folded hands over her belly while she watched the sky. She didn't have to turn her head to know Cash was frowning.

"Only because he has a property between two lakes," Will said, bringing more beers out to nestle into a cooler filled with ice. "If we didn't already have houses, any one of us could have done something like this."

"Yeah, but you didn't." Gavin shot Hallie a wink. She loved him cocky and overly confident. She couldn't help herself.

"But I like where we live," Hannah argued. Her

hands rested on her own belly, and Hallie knew what was under those hands. Her twin sister had found out she was pregnant a few days ago. She was seven weeks along. She'd told everyone right away.

Hallie was rounding her final month, and her due date couldn't come fast enough. She was going to have two very large baby boys. She had agreed with the doctor that a C-section was the way to go. But her sons weren't ready to come out yet, no matter how anxious she and Gavin were to meet them.

"How much longer until fireworks?" Cassandra asked, opening a beer for herself. She and Luke were getting married in a few months. They were waiting to start a family until after the wedding. Presley and Cash, though, hadn't waited until they were married. After a small ceremony on the dock, Pres confessed she was already eight weeks along.

Hallie and Gavin's twin boys would have plenty of cousins to play with, that was for sure.

"It has to be dark for fireworks, sweetheart," Luke told his fiancée. "It's only dusk."

Cassandra sighed. "Regardless, I'd rather await fireworks in Gavin and Hallie's backyard. This is so much better than spending an evening at Mags Dumond's soiree. I'm glad we skipped it."

"Hear, hear," Presley agreed. "Let's be the generation that *doesn't* show up at parties we don't want to attend."

"I will drink to that." Gavin leaned forward to tap his beer can to his brothers' beer cans.

Hallie lifted her water bottle. "Me, too."

"Everything that's important is right here, right

now," Gavin announced, reaching for Hallie's hand. He kissed her ear and whispered, "I love you."

"I love you, too," she whispered back.

"Were we that gross?" Will asked, and Hannah laughed.

"Worse," Cash answered, and Presley laughed.

What might've turned into a brotherly argument was interrupted by the night's first firework exploding overhead. Colorful sparks rained down as everyone clapped.

Hallie, her palms resting on her very pregnant belly, felt her babies kick. "They liked that."

Another firework streaked the night sky. Gavin's hand joined hers on her belly and they locked eyes as their sons gave a few more exuberant kicks.

Any moment now, they would arrive on this plane and usher in a new generation. One that would forever intertwine the branches of the Banks and Sutherland family trees.

As Hallie looked around at the faces lit by bright fireworks overhead, she had to smile. She'd never imagined this life for herself, but here it was. As big and bold and beautiful as Gavin had promised.

All she had to do was let go…

And break a few rules.

* * * * *

Look for the next Dynasties!

Dynasties: The Carey Center
from USA TODAY *bestselling author*
Maureen Child

Available October 2021

WE HOPE YOU ENJOYED
THIS BOOK FROM

DESIRE

*Luxury, scandal, desire—welcome to
the lives of the American elite.*

Be transported to the worlds of oil barons, family dynasties,
moguls and celebrities. Get ready for juicy plot twists,
delicious sensuality and intriguing scandal.

6 NEW BOOKS AVAILABLE EVERY MONTH!

COMING NEXT MONTH FROM

DESIRE

#2821 HOW TO CATCH A BAD BOY
Texas Cattleman's Club: Heir Apparent • by Cat Schield
Private Investigator Lani Li must get up close and personal with her
onetime lover, former playboy Asher Edmond, who's accused of
embezzling—and insists he's innocent. With suspicions—and chemistry—
building, can she get the job done without losing her heart a second time?

#2822 SECRETS OF A ONE NIGHT STAND
Billionaires of Boston • by Naima Simone
After one hot night with a handsome stranger, business executive
Mycah Hill doesn't expect to see him again. Then she starts her new job
and he's her *boss*, CEO Achilles Farrell. But keeping things professional
is hard when she learns she's having his child...

#2823 BLIND DATE WITH THE SPARE HEIR
Locketts of Tuxedo Park • by Yahrah St. John
Elyse Robinson believes the powerful Lockett family swindled her father.
And when her blind date is second son Dr. Julian Lockett, it's her chance
to find the family's weaknesses—but it turns out Julian is *her*
weakness. With sparks flying, will she choose love or loyalty?

#2824 THE FAKE ENGAGEMENT FAVOR
The Texas Tremaines • by Charlene Sands
When country music superstar Gage Tremaine's reputation is rocked by
scandal, he needs a fake fiancée fast to win back fans. Family friend and
former nemesis college professor Gianna Marino is perfect for the role—
until their very real chemistry becomes impossible to ignore...

#2825 WAYS TO TEMPT THE BOSS
Brooklyn Nights • by Joanne Rock
CEO Lucas Deschamps needs to protect his family's cosmetics business
by weeding out a corporate spy, and he suspects new employee
Blair Wescott. He's determined to find the truth by getting closer to her—
but the heat between them may be a temptation he can't resist...

#2826 BEST LAID WEDDING PLANS
Moonlight Ridge • by Karen Booth
Resort wedding planner Autumn Kincaid is a hopeless romantic even
after being left at the altar. Grey Holloway is Mr. Grump and a new
partner in the resort. Now that he's keeping an eye on her, sparks ignite,
but will their differences derail everything?

YOU CAN FIND MORE INFORMATION ON UPCOMING HARLEQUIN TITLES,
FREE EXCERPTS AND MORE AT HARLEQUIN.COM.

HDCNM0821

*After one hot night with a handsome stranger, business
executive Mycah Hill doesn't expect to see him again.
Then she starts her new job and he's her boss,
CEO Achilles Farrell. But keeping things professional
is hard when she learns she's having his child...*

Read on for a sneak peek at
Secrets of a One Night Stand
by USA TODAY *bestselling author Naima Simone.*

"You're staring again."

"I am." Mycah switched her legs, recrossing them. And damn his too-observant gaze, he didn't miss the gesture. Probably knew why she did it, too. Not that the action alleviated the sweet pain pulsing inside her. "Does it still bother you?"

"Depends."

"On?"

"Why you're staring."

She slicked the tip of her tongue over her lips, an unfamiliar case of nerves making themselves known. Again, his eyes caught the tell, dropping to her mouth, resting there, and the blast of heat that exploded inside her damn near fused her to the bar stool. What he did with one look... Jesus, it wasn't fair. Not to her. Not to humankind.

"Because you're so stareable. Don't do that," she insisted, no, *implored* when he stiffened, his eyes going glacial. Frustration stormed inside her, swirling and releasing in a sharp clap of laughter. She huffed out a breath, shaking her head. "You should grant me leeway because you don't know me, and I don't know you. And you, all of you—" she waved her hand up and down, encompassing his long, below-the-shoulder-length hair, his massive shoulders, his thick thighs and his large booted feet "—are a lot."

"A lot of what?" His body didn't loosen, his face remaining shuttered. But that voice...

She shivered. It had deepened to a growl, and her breath caught.

"A lot of—" she spread out her arms the length of his shoulders "—mass. A lot of attitude." She exhaled, her hands dropping to her thighs. "A lot of beauty," she murmured, and it contained a slight tremble she hated but couldn't erase. "A lot of pride. A lot of…" Fire. Darkness. Danger. Shelter.

Her fingers curled into her palm.

"A lot of intensity," she finished. Lamely. Jesus, so lamely.

Achilles stared at her. And she fought not to fidget under his hooded gaze. Struggled to remain still as he leaned forward and that tantalizing, woodsy scent beckoned her closer seconds before he did.

"Mycah, come here."

She should be rebelling; she should be stiffening in offense at that rumbled order. Should be. But no. Instead, a weight she hadn't consciously been aware of tumbled off her shoulders. Allowing her to breathe deeper…freer. Because as Achilles gripped the lapel of her jacket and drew her closer, wrinkling the silk, he also slowly peeled away Mycah Hill, the business executive who helmed and carried the responsibilities of several departments… Mycah Hill, the eldest daughter of Laurence and Cherise Hill, who bore the burden of their financial irresponsibility and unrealistic expectations.

In their place stood Mycah, the vulnerable stripped-bare woman who wanted to let go. Who *could* let go. Just this once.

So as he reeled her in, she went, willingly, until their faces hovered barely an inch apart. Until their breaths mingled. Until his bright gaze heated her skin.

This close, she glimpsed the faint smattering of freckles across the tops of his lean cheeks and the high bridge of his nose. The light cinnamon spots should've detracted from the sensual brutality of his features. But they didn't. In an odd way, they enhanced it.

Had her wanting to dot each one with the top of her tongue.

"What?" she whispered.

"Say it again." He released her jacket and trailed surprisingly gentle fingers up her throat. "I want to find out for myself what the lie tastes like on your mouth."

Lust flashed inside her, hot, searing. Consuming.

God, she liked it. This…*consuming*.

If she wasn't careful, she could easily come to crave it.

Don't miss what happens next in…
Secrets of a One Night Stand *by Naima Simone,*
the next book in the Billionaires of Boston series!

Available September 2021 wherever
Harlequin Desire books and ebooks are sold.

Harlequin.com

Get 4 FREE REWARDS!

We'll send you 2 FREE Books plus 2 FREE Mystery Gifts.

Harlequin Desire books transport you to the world of the American elite with juicy plot twists, delicious sensuality and intriguing scandal.

FREE
Value Over
$20

Love Harlequin romance?

DISCOVER.

Be the first to find out about promotions, news and exclusive content!

- Facebook.com/HarlequinBooks
- Twitter.com/HarlequinBooks
- Instagram.com/HarlequinBooks
- Pinterest.com/HarlequinBooks
- YouTube.com/HarlequinBooks

ReaderService.com

EXPLORE.

Sign up for the Harlequin e-newsletter and download a free book from any series at **TryHarlequin.com**

CONNECT.

Join our Harlequin community to share your thoughts and connect with other romance readers!
Facebook.com/groups/HarlequinConnection

HARLEQUIN